The Extraordinary Curiosities of Ixworth & Maddox

This is a work of fiction. Names, characters, places, and incidents either are the product of the author's imagination or are used fictitiously. Any resemblance to actual persons, living or dead, events, or locales is entirely coincidental.

First paperback edition May 2023

Cover illustration by Paulina Wyrt

www.jdgrolic.com

THE Extraordinary Curiosities OF IXWORTH & MADDOX

J.D. GROLIC

CHAPTER 1

THE EXTRAORDINARY CURIOSITIES OF IXWORTH AND MADDOX

The sign on the shop front read:

Opening Soon
The Extraordinary Curiosities of Ixworth & Maddox.
Hours: Monday to Friday: 12:00–17:00.
Appointments: 17:30–20:30.
Saturday and Sunday: 10:00–15:00.
Appointments: 16:00–18:30

It was written in a tidy, delicate script, a clue that those who owned the business were intent on offering only the finest quality goods.

The shop, a well-kept building of grey brick with

a slightly lopsided roof, was owned exclusively by one of the gentlemen listed on the shopfront sign: a Mr. R. Maddox, the name which—remarkably—had been on the deed to the property, #17 South Molton Lane, Mayfield, London, United Kingdom, for one hundred and eleven years.

For those unfamiliar with the layout of London Streets, South Molten *Lane* runs in an east-westerly direction one block south of the flashier South Molton *Street*, which is home to some of London's finest shops. Two places with names nearly the same, yet as different as night and day.

South Molton *Street* is posh and stylish, visited by artists, oil barons, television personalities, and those used to getting what they want. South Molton *Lane* is its opposite: a simple alleyway to some, not even a street at all to others. A small place tucked well out of the way of the bustle of other more famous routes. Yet to those with a nose for such things, South Molton Lane has an energy all its own.

For many years, *the Extraordinary Curiosities of Ixworth and Maddox* wasn't a curiosity shop at all but was a shop run by an herbalist from Ipswich who rented the space from Mr. Maddox. It had been an honest business, complete with an overweight tabby named Liquorice, who had a habit of dozing with his fat bottom pressed flat against the front window display. The shop had been a neighbourhood fixture with quality goods at fair prices, a helpful and kind owner, and excellent customer service, yet it never really found success. Regrettably, this story is not about an Ipswich herbalist. He went out of business. And he moved to Buckingham after meeting a sweet and sour woman named RoseMary at a police auction.

Number 17 sat empty and abandoned for many years and fell into disrepair, as things lonely and forgotten often do. Its cheerful exterior grew shoddy and tired. There were rumours it had become a meeting place for hermits. Locals gossiped it was the clubhouse of a sinister gang where men in dark suits gathered to carry out mischief and all kinds of evil deeds not worth mentioning within these pages.

And yet, London realms change: lanes are reversed, one-way streets become thoroughfares, broadways are opened, passages and secret walkways are forgotten, pavement is moved, shouldered left or right. Buildings rocket skyward; others come down. Life forgets the past and races forward to accept the future. Just so, change came to South Molton Lane, for one blustery Friday in January, someone returned to claim the abandoned shop.

The shopfront underwent a remarkable transformation.

At first, the changes to the outside were minor: small adjustments only someone familiar with the area would notice, like the ageing of one's own face. Door trim restored; the store entranceway cleared and swept of rubbish; blinds put up; the old herbalist sign taken down. As time passed, the changes became more noticeable: windows were replaced; cracked bricks repaired, the roof re-tarred. By the middle of February, the shop was near unrecognisable from the rundown place of old. Strangely, and much to the surprise (and concern) of the business owners in the neighbourhood, all of these repairs—even the large ones—seemed to occur after dark, for no one living or working in the area of South Molton Lane could ever remember seeing any workmen about the shop during the day.

One could ask the nosy retailer from the antique shop across the lane, the one who went out for a newspaper on the first day of March and noticed the shop's door had been painted the colour of a ripe plum—he could've sworn it had been a dull grey the day before. Or ask the Oxford Street chocolate maker who always chained her bike inside the South Molton Passage—she noticed the shop window, which had been covered in old newspapers for as long as she could remember, was now clear and shone like a brightly lit stage overlooking the lane.

Yet, by far the most mysterious thing about the newly renovated South Molton Lane shop (henceforth known as *the Extraordinary Curiosities of Ixworth and Maddox*) were the two strange gentlemen who appeared to own it.

The first of these two, Mr. Ixworth, was a short, slightly ruffled fellow who had one of those funny *I've a bit of chocolate on my lip* moustaches. He said little and talked with few, but when he did speak, his thoughts were measured and wise. He seemed a man at ease; he held a calm about him that was difficult to put to words.

The second man, Mr. Maddox, was handsome for

his years. He was polite and sincere yet not one to use one word when two would do. His bustling, dithery personality was a sign of his terrific talent for chitchat (no matter what the subject). Mr. Maddox was a people person, and once settled in the neighbourhood, he became known to all. Yet, despite his outgoing and easy manner, many who had dealings with Mr. Maddox often suspected he was a man with a secret. And indeed he was.

How Chloe Ashley—a normal, everyday girl who went to school, rode the bus, did chores and loved books—came to be friends with Mr. Ixworth and Mr. Maddox is a tale, like many, born from a single coincidental moment.

Chloe's story begins on an April Thursday, a day some would call ordinary—which is a silly thing to say, for London is no ordinary city, and even the most boring day in London is an extraordinary one. A person need only walk its streets to get a sense of its history. And for those with a keener sense, its *magic*. For there are a good many magical things both above and below London's tangled streets and alleyways. But magic was far from the thoughts of eleven-year-old Chloe as she walked along busy Brook Street. She was thinking about her troubles, for she had just had the worst day of her life.

"Here's some pocket money," Mum had said that morning, sliding two crisp bills toward Chloe as she was eating breakfast at the kitchen table. "This should last you the week. Don't spend it all at once, and make sure you lock the door when you leave, okay?"

Chloe stopped, a spoonful of cereal poised between

mouth and bowl, milk dripping like pearly teardrops. "I thought Dad was taking me to school?" she said.

"He's already left," said Mum distractedly. "Something about a meeting. So-and-so from the accounting office. You have your Oyster Card?"

"Of course," said Chloe. "How would I get to school without it?"

Chloe pushed her breakfast away and watched Mum collect her things in a whirlwind of measured movements: dashing about in her new suit, gathering papers and housekeys, checking the contents of her briefcase with care. The night before, Dad had made an unusual offer after hearing Chloe had gotten an A on her history project. "That's my clever Chlo," he'd said, folding his newspaper. "How about I drive you to school in the morning? No sense you getting up early to catch that bus. This can be your, *hrmm*, reward."

It was typical for Dad not to keep a promise. He was always forgetting about Chloe: unsigned tests; a late pickup after the cinema; a missed permission form for a field trip to the London Transport Museum that Chloe had been desperate to attend. Mum wasn't much better: on Chloe's last birthday, Mum had presented her with a candled cake covered in almonds. Chloe had just rolled her eyes. She was allergic to nuts!

Chloe got up from the kitchen table to pour her leftover milk down the sink. She tried to push her bitterness aside. It was a regular struggle between her two selves. There was a part of her, not the average, pale lanky girl with dark hair that everyone saw on the outside, but a separate, reasonable self, who knew why she had to come home to an empty house. This mature half understood why it was necessary for her to make her own dinners and put herself to bed. Her parents weren't bad. On the contrary, they provided a comfortable home; they never yelled or got especially angry, nor did they force her to live beneath a staircase or cooped away in some dingy attic. Perhaps Mr. and Mrs. Ashley's only failing—a problem that probably affects parents the world over—was they were busy.

Too busy for her.

Mr. Ashley was a manager for a very old, very snooty, privately-owned bank. During the week, he acted like a strange faraway spirit who only talked to Chloe and Mum by telephone. His calls usually came around six o'clock, his words like a list of bullet points: Filing. Editing papers. Completing forms.

Like Mr. Ashley, Mrs. Ashley had a busy job. She was an up-and-coming agent at Wilbur and Smithers Estate Agents and Premium Letting Services. She was away nearly as much as Dad thanks to a hectic schedule of home showings.

Chloe tugged on her backpack and slumped off to school.

Iris Sturgeon was Chloe's best friend. They had grown up together on the same street and had gone to the same schools since they were three. When Mum and Dad bought the house on Wood's Mews and her family had moved from Lisson Grove, Chloe had made a pact with Iris to remain friends. But there were times Chloe felt Iris was growing up faster than she was. Iris's bubbly personality made it easy for her to make friends, which often made Chloe jealous.

"What's wrong with you?" said Iris as they emerged into the hallway after second period. "You didn't say a word the entire class."

Chloe had been feeling quieter than usual. "Nothing. Just bored. I guess?"

Iris shouldered her schoolbag, leading the way into the busy hallway. "Do you want to come to my house after school?"

Chloe was about to say yes when they were suddenly interrupted by two girls who stopped to ask Iris something. Chloe waved to them shyly but didn't speak.

"So?" said Iris after the girls had gone. "Coming over?"

"Of course," said Chloe. "Why?"

"Just wondering," said Iris. "I've asked Olivia and Sophie to come too. You remember them? We were going to watch this new show Sophie and I found over the weekend."

Chloe had been in the same class as Sophie the previous year. She was funny and outgoing. All the boys in her year were always talking about her. "Oh? Them?"

Iris frowned. "They're fun. You like them."

Chloe was used to Iris surprising her, but today it seemed annoying. "We did something with Olivia last week," said Chloe. "I thought it was just going to be you and me today?"

Iris rolled her eyes. "Oh, Chloe. You always do this."

"Always do what?" Chloe snapped.

"This. What you're doing. It's like you don't want to be friends with anybody."

Chloe was about to say something else but closed her mouth. Iris was right. Struggling for her friend's attention in groups made Chloe tired. Half the time she ended up not saying anything at all.

"I do," she muttered.

Iris gave Chloe a chilly stare. "Well, it's up to you. If you don't want to come, you don't have to." She walked away.

Chloe was late getting to her next class. Mr. Barnes, the mathematics teacher, had a thing for punctuality. He didn't take kindly to stragglers.

"Sorry everyone," announced Mr. Barnes as she came in, "I'll pause our lesson now. *Chloe* has arrived. Welcome, Chloe. Thank you for attending my class. We'll just wait while you find your seat. Take your time."

Chloe slunk to her desk. Around her, many of her classmates were trying to conceal their laughter. Brice Sadberry, the wickedest boy in Chloe's year, snorted and pointed. Chloe sunk low in her chair, face red.

Last period didn't get any better. Chloe scored poorly on her musical assessment and would need to write it again. When the bell finally rang, she waited for everyone to clear from the classroom before she packed up her things.

Chloe messaged Iris on her mobile. "Mum said

I have to come home after school," she lied. "Maybe tomorrow?"

Iris responded almost immediately. "K."

Chloe immediately felt bad but didn't feel up to apologising. Sometimes saying sorry was hard, especially when she was still feeling hurt. Thankfully, the bus wasn't full when Chloe boarded outside the school. She found a seat near the back and put her head down against the window. At George Street, she was distracted by a group of girls walking on the pavement beside the bus, Iris among them. Olivia and Sophie tagged behind her chatting. A rotten finish to an already rotten day.

She got off the bus in a dark mood. Somebody was honking a car horn more times than necessary. Why were London drivers so impatient? As she rounded a corner onto South Molton Lane, Chloe decided she would visit her favourite bookstore that afternoon. She wanted to take Mum's instructions seriously and not spend all of her pocket money. She didn't want to be one of those children who ignore everything their parents said. But Chloe loved books above all else. Reading would be a welcome distraction and a way to forget what had happened at school. Chloe cringed just thinking about it.

The bookstore was warm and welcoming, and soon she was paying for an intriguing new mystery. When she got home, she would curl up in her room and forget. As she neared Davis Street, a grape-size raindrop hit her nose. A backdrop of dark clouds had begun to descend on Mayfair at great speed. Her house was a few blocks away. If the rain would just hold off a bit longer, she might make it home without getting drenched.

As if answering a dare, the clouds began to dispense a torrent of plump raindrops. In only a few short moments, the narrow lane ran deep with rainwater and Chloe was soaked. Fearing for the contents of her rucksack Chloe ducked into the narrow doorway to number 17.

The space offered little shelter. Turning her back to the street, she noted the *opening soon* sign that had been tacked to the door. Beyond the smoked glass, a light was on. To her left, a curtain had been drawn across the window display, but a sliver of light poked out into the darkening street. Chloe wiped her breath from the pane, and a fresh gust of wind splattered raindrops onto her back. She could make a dash for the antique market, but her rucksack was soggy as it was. Number 17 was her best option. Perhaps the owner wouldn't mind if she waited out the rain inside. She grabbed the door handle. It was warm. For a moment, she thought she could feel a tremor, like a pulse coursing into her hand. Setting her uneasiness aside, she pushed the door open, and a flurry of angry rain compelled her inside.

Chloe closed the door behind her. The sound of the rain grew quiet, like someone drawing a bath in a faraway room. She stood for a moment, drip-dripping on a doormat. The shop was small, and its dim interior had a cosy charm. A high ceiling had been fitted with hanging lights in the shape of dark starlit tulips that cast a pleasing light on the wide hardwood planks below. To the rear of the shop, beside a doorway that led away to a darkened storeroom, was a chunky wooden countertop; an old-fashioned cash register sat near its open end.

The shop's most noticeable feature was a raised stage showcasing an assortment of rare oddities—a handsome puppet theatre with mulberry curtains, the backdrop painted with summer hills and a wide-faced moon. Chloe had never been one for stuffed animals—or dolls, for that matter—but the allure of the tiny theatre was undeniable. Beside it lay a collection of dazzling hand-painted paper fortune tellers depicting enchanted animals: reindeer walking upright and tigers dressed in robes of purple and silver, each waiting for a child's frantic fingers. There were other sights—so many enchanting things to behold! A model railroad running on a wide loop of track; a spooky casket coin box, wherein one could place a coin at the short end and a skeleton's hand would emerge from a trap and draw the coin within; a circus-themed jack-in-the-box; painted teapots in the shape of mushroom houses; framed maps of countries unknown (where was the Land of Hobb?).

Yet, it wasn't the amazing merchandise, nor the cosy interior, nor the shop's smell of wood, old books and caramel reminiscent of a kindly grandmother's kitchen that had Chloe awestruck. It was the extraordinary spectacle in front of her. Tiny, man-like creatures dressed in colourful tunics and breeches and well-buckled boots were nipping about in pairs, to and fro, setting up, sweeping, tidying. Small pale forms with delicate features and large heads. Bright wide eyes and pointed ears, a slender line for a nose. Each beautiful, yet with a sameness that made them hard to tell apart. Some of them had bewitched the merchandise—or so it seemed—for a gleaming accordion and an old fashioned ice-cream maker were floating above their heads, guided by little hands toward the display.

Who could blame Chloe for staring at the tiny feet scurrying to set up the shop? Or the nimble hands holding tiny tools? For it was an uncommon sight that only a handful of people in London's long history have ever seen, the sort of tiny beings one would expect to see popping out beneath a misty-toed elm of Hyde Park or slipping silently out of St. Pancras's narrower alleyways or some other black corner of the city. Brownies are renowned for their secretive ways, after all.

Chloe gaped.

Everything—object, broom, cloth, mop–stopped. The accordion and ice cream maker sank gently to the floor.

For a moment there was a standoff in the tiny shop: wide-eyed Chloe staring at the busyness of brownies; the brownies staring back, alarm fresh on their faces. Chloe flinched, and the brownies scattered, cramming through the door to the rear of the shop in a quick and disorderly line. Chloe made a frantic turn, wanting very much to be out and away, but somebody was blocking the exit. A short, slightly ruffled fellow with one of those funny *I've a bit of chocolate on my lip* moustaches.

"I'm afraid I can't let you leave," said the man.

CHAPTER 2

IXWORTH AND MADDOX

"May I ask how you got in here?" inquired the moustached man in a quiet tone.

Chloe took a step back from the door. "I was trying to get out of the rain," she said uneasily.

"Hrrrm," said the man. "That's not exactly what I asked." He looked at the shop door before speaking again. "I mean: how did you open this door?"

Chloe noted the man's untidy appearance: A tweed jacket two sizes too large, ruffled trousers, thinning hair, a wide mouth. Yet he had a pleasant way about him, the way a charming uncle might seem.

"It was unlocked," she said flatly.

"Unlocked?" said the man, blinking.

"Yes," said Chloe.

"I locked it myself."

"Maybe the lock's broken," Chloe offered.

The man thought about this. "I doubt the lock is the problem."

"I just wanted to be somewhere dry."

"And here you are."

Chloe eyed the door, wanting very much to be on the other side looking in. "I'm sorry," she said. "I'll leave now."

The man held his arm out, barring the way. "One moment, please. I can't let you go until we get to the bottom of this."

"Get to the bottom of what?" said Chloe, and it was about then she realised she might be in trouble.

"Just a few more questions," the man said calmly, holding up his hands in a non-threatening manner. "No reason to be alarmed. I just need to know if someone sent you."

"I don't know what you mean," said Chloe.

"Sent to spy? That sort of thing?"

"Of course not!" said Chloe. "This is … I don't even know what kind of place this is."

"It's only the finest shop in London," a new voice broke in excitedly, "where people of fine taste come to buy the highest quality knick-knacks and rarities, obviously. Or didn't you notice the fabulous display?"

Chloe whirled around. Another man had come in from the rear of the shop and was standing behind the chunky counter. "I'm afraid this is my doing," he said to no one in particular. "I poked my head out a little while ago for a taste of air. Funny how a bit of London atmosphere can be refreshing. I must have forgotten to lock the door after I came back in."

The moustached man shook his head and tutted. "I've told you a thousand times, Maddox."

The other man, Mr. Maddox, came around the counter with a look of concern. He was dressed in a trim suit of grey. A grape-coloured bowtie was tied neatly about his neck, and his pointy shoes were polished black. He was a good head taller than his companion.

"My apologies, everyone," he said. "My fault. Deeply, deeply sorry and all that."

"Only minor harm done," muttered the moustached man.

"Well?" said Mr. Maddox, "Are we all just going to stand here playing silly whatsits? I think introductions are in order: I am Mr. Maddox. My quiet associate, whom you've already met, is Mr. Ixworth. This is our curiosity shop. And you are?"

It took a few breaths before Chloe could speak. Being questioned by grown-ups was frightening.

"Chloe," said Chloe.

"Chloe what?" said Mr. Maddox.

"Ashley," said Chloe, not wanting to be impolite.

"Nice to meet you," said Mr. Maddox cheerily.

The cause of Chloe's anxiety came rushing back to mind: "What were those things?" she blurted.

"What *things?*" said Mr. Maddox.

"Those, little—men," said Chloe.

"Oh, them," said Mr. Maddox. "Our helpers?"

Mr. Ixworth cleared his throat. "Perhaps we shouldn't be talking about this with strangers," he said, looking pointedly at his partner.

"Talking about what?" Mr. Maddox said mildly.

He turned to Chloe: "Miss, are you sure you weren't imagining these little men?"

"How did they make those things float like that?" said Chloe, and then having asked, she suddenly worried she had seen something she wasn't supposed to.

Mr. Maddox sighed. "I guess it was too much to hope for. Cat's out of the bag." He paused, looking at Chloe closely. "They were brownies. And they were using magic. A curiosities shop wouldn't be much good without magic, now would it?"

Mr. Ixworth raised an eyebrow. "I might have offered some other explanation, Maddox," he said. "Are you trying to give us away?"

"Now let's be rational, Ixworth," said Mr. Maddox. "How much has she really seen? A brownie? Three? One busyness? Even if she decided to tell her parents, friends, teachers, what-have-yous, who would believe her? Brownies, running about a shop in present-day London? Casting spells and using potions? Rubbish. I don't believe it myself!"

Mr. Ixworth studied them for a moment. "I suppose what's done cannot be undone," he said finally.

"That's the spirit, old boy," said Mr. Maddox gently. "Now, I think we should let this young lady be on her way. I'll put the tea on and we can turn our minds to work. Opening day is fast approaching."

For a moment, nobody spoke, each of them still and solemn.

Chloe took a step, fearing Mr. Ixworth and Mr. Maddox might change their minds. Both men watched her intently. She moved slowly at first, tiptoeing toward the door. Upon reaching it, she pulled it wide, then with one last look back, she hurried out into the soggy street.

"Please come back soon," called Mr. Maddox.

But Chloe couldn't hear. Wild feet had carried her away.

✦ ✦ ✦

That night, Chloe couldn't sleep. The events at the shop had left her in a tizzy of excited emotions. It was like someone had told her Christmas had been moved to tomorrow. She had been a little scared of Mr. Ixworth at first, yet learning there were brownies alive and living right here in London made the discomfort worth it. What had Mr. Maddox said? A curiosity shop wouldn't be much good without magic? It wasn't every day one discovered magic was real. Really-real.

Chloe spent much of the next day at school daydreaming and wondering if there were other magical beasts running about that she should know about. Ogres? Werewolves? What was the plural of Sasquatch? When the school bell rang at 3:15, she was starting to second-guess her memories. She had even begun to wonder if the shop was real. Maybe she had made it all up? There was only one way to find out! Chloe didn't return home directly after school. Instead, she made her way to *the Extraordinary Curiosities of Ixworth and Maddox*.

As she entered, a doorbell sang happily: a clear

chime like sleigh bells. The shop was deserted. Chloe ran a hand across the smooth wood of the counter. Near the door, something new had been added to the display: A miniature model building. It was about the size of a desk lamp with lines of tiny windows across its front. Some of the windows were alight, allowing Chloe to see into the tiny lives of the building's residents: an elderly couple reading beneath the glow of a lamp; a man in a robe and shower cap brushing his teeth in front of a mirror; a young family crowded around a kitchen table; a cat alone on a sofa. Chloe would later discover there was a key at the side of the building. If it were wound, a tiny wooden man would move along the length of the structure, popping up in open door frames in the hallway, winding his way up a staircase to the top floor. Once there, he would descend again by some unseen way, finishing up in his original position at the base. Chloe was entranced.

"Well, I can't say I'm surprised to see you again," said a familiar voice. Chloe turned to see Mr. Ixworth enter from the rear of the shop. He was dressed in a tweed jacket, different than the day before, yet just as ruffled.

"Sorry," Chloe said nervously. "I wasn't snooping. There was no one about."

"I didn't think you were," said Mr. Ixworth, matter-of-factly. He paused, assessing her. "You don't seem the snooping sort. What can I help you with?"

Chloe glanced at the floor. "I just popped by to say hi—uh, I really like your display," she said awkwardly, pointing toward the tiny building. "How long have you and Mr. Maddox been working together on ... on this?"

Mr. Ixworth folded his hands neatly in front of him. "Hrrm. If memory serves me correctly, we've been friends since the spring of 1928. But this shop will be the first time we've run a business together."

Chloe did a rough calculation in her head. "That was ninety years ago," she said, suddenly wondering if Mr. Ixworth was teasing her. "Um. That's a long time."

"Indeed it is," said Mr. Maddox, suddenly entering from the rear of the shop. He was dressed impeccably in tailored pants and a patterned navy vest. "We met in Covent Garden Market. I had put down a bundle of rare radishes to look at something from another seller. Ixworth came along and scooped them up. Not that I blame him. Good radishes are hard to find, you see. When I realised he had taken them, I was not pleased. Not. At. All. I followed him all the way to Drury Lane to give him a piece of my mind. Finders are finders, I always say. He had the nerve to vex me with an *Accumulation*. Bold-bold-bold." Mr. Maddox paused in the telling of his tale, to give Chloe a wink. "We've been friends ever since."

"*Accumulation?*" said Chloe, "I have no idea what that means."

"Right, right," said Mr. Maddox, looking thoughtful. "I guess you wouldn't."

"And how were you both alive in 1928?" said Chloe. "You don't look ..." she paused. More maths. It wasn't her strongest subject.

"I think she's calling us old," said Mr. Ixworth, "or young? I'm not sure which."

"Never met a magician before, have you?" said Mr. Maddox.

"No," said Chloe uncertainty, "unless you count that American guy on television. The one who makes things disappear. I saw one of his shows when I was a kid."

Mr. Maddox gave Chloe a look like he had been forced to swallow raw broccoli. "That's not real magic," he said.

"Oh," said Chloe, feeling she had hurt Mr. Maddox's feelings. "I'm sorry, I guess I don't know the difference. What kinds of tricks do real magicians do?"

"You think we just do tricks?" said Mr. Maddox. "You have trouble believing we do real magic?"

"I'm still not sure," said Chloe shakily. "Your brownies were making a lot of things float around. I … well, I'm not sure what I should think. Everything is just so mad."

"Perfect!" clucked Mr. Maddox. "Exactly what we want to hear. Magicians welcome doubt. Encourage it, actually. Keeps people off our scent, so to speak."

"So that bit about meeting Mr. Ixworth all those years ago?" said Chloe. "That's not true, then?"

Mr. Maddox was taken aback. "My dear," he said, "we wouldn't have to be magicians to have been alive in 1928. It was only ninety years ago."

"But you don't look anywhere near ninety," said Chloe, looking at him.

"Thank you," Mr. Maddox said with a slight bow. "It does a man good to hear he looks less than his years."

"And how old is that?" said Chloe, forgetting how rude she sounded.

"That old fool is a lot older than ninety," said Mr. Ixworth.

"How is that possible?" said Chloe. "He looks the same age as my dad."

"Like I said," replied Mr. Maddox, "I'm a magician."

"I suppose you have a magic wand then?" teased Chloe, who was starting to feel strangely at ease with two self-proclaimed magicians.

"Tut-tut, Miss Ashley," said Mr. Ixworth. "Real magicians are different from the ones in storybooks."

"So, how do you do magic?" said Chloe.

It was Mr. Maddox who answered, for the matter of magic clearly needed a lengthy explanation. Mr. Ixworth seemed happy to let his partner speak. "To put it simply," said Mr. Maddox, "the business of magic, in other words, creating potions, elixirs, laves and casting spells, is ultimately tied to the place it started: a magician's realm."

"Realm?" said Chloe frowning. "Like, where you live? This shop?"

"In a way," said Mr. Maddox, "but it's more than just this shop. In fact, Mayfair is my realm."

"All of Mayfair?" said Chloe.

"Not all," said Mr. Maddox, "but a good portion: Green Park to Paddington. West Soho to the tail of the Serpentine. The exception is Shepherd Market. That's taken."

"I don't understand," said Chloe.

"I know it seems a difficult thing to understand," said Mr. Maddox. "Put simply: magicians are bound to their place. Our magic stems from a deep connection to our realm. This shop hasn't been around all that long, but I've governed Mayfair since the late 1700s."

Chloe, who had read her share of books, found that hard to believe. "What happens if you leave?" she asked.

Mr. Maddox shook his head sadly. "Should I venture beyond my borders, I would lose many of my abilities. Venture outside my realm for too long, and well ... what's the term they use? Pushing-up daisies?"

"You'll die if you leave Mayfair?" asked Chloe.

"Oh no-no-no," cried Mr. Maddox. "Not right away. It would take some time." He held an arm out toward Mr. Ixworth. "Ixworth leaves his realm to come work at this shop but returns home most evenings. He's not affected."

"So these realms, as you call them, keep you young, or do you all just live forever?" asked Chloe.

"True to a degree," said Mr. Maddox. "One can use magic to slow down the ageing process. But, magician or not, we're all bound by the rules of mortality."

Mr. Ixworth came to stand behind the register. He examined Chloe for a moment. "Can I ask you something?" he said.

"Yes. Anything," said Chloe.

"You wouldn't happen to have any magicians in your family, would you Miss Ashley?"

"Of course not," said Chloe, who had no reason to believe anyone from her family besides a misbehaved cousin or two on Dad's side was anything but ordinary. "Why?"

"You just have a look about you, that's all," said Mr. Ixworth thoughtfully. "I recall thinking the same thing when you first came into the shop the other day. Just a quick little thing that popped into my head: There's something about this young lady that's special."

CHAPTER 3

THE SPOTTER'S SKY TAXI

The next time Chloe stopped by the curiosity shop, the sleigh bell door chime was silent. For a moment, she thought she had lost her hearing, for she could clearly see the chime hanging above the door like mistletoe, ready to greet any and all who crossed the threshold. Chloe pushed the door back and forth, open, closed, in an attempt to make them speak.

"The bell only greets strangers," said Ixworth, who was behind the counter hanging a series of framed black and white ink drawings of plants. "Thank you for testing them. It's always best when customers announce themselves. Wouldn't want anything getting pinched."

"Do you have any customers?" said Chloe. "I don't think I've ever seen one."

"Not many," said Ixworth. "It's best if we magicians keep to ourselves and our business ventures a secret. We sell non-magical items during the day. Magical offerings are available for our evening appointments."

"Magical items?" said Chloe. The things already on display seemed magical enough.

"Yes. Magical items are our specialty," said Ixworth. "We don't expect much business during the day. It's more of a cover, really."

"But who will buy your ... magical stuff if nobody is supposed to know about you?"

Mr. Ixworth gave Chloe a puzzled look. "Other magicians of course."

Chloe had no time to ask anything further. There was a sudden ring at the door, and a man in a floppy hat entered the shop. Chloe and Ixworth looked at each other in unison.

"See?" said Ixworth cheekily. "We have customers." He nodded his head to one side. "There's a stool behind the counter beside the register. Why don't you have a seat while I help this gentleman?"

Chloe did as she was asked, happy to have more time in the shop. She set her rucksack behind the counter and took a seat on the wide stool. The man in the hat was searching for a birthday present for his niece. Ixworth made a few polite suggestions but kept his distance while the man looked over the curiosities on display.

"Oh? Look who's come by to mind our little shop," said Maddox, who breezed in quite suddenly from the door behind the register.

Chloe wasn't surprised, for it seemed Maddox was always waiting just inside the rear entrance in case an opportunity arose for him to make a grand entrance.

"Yes, it's me," said Chloe.

Maddox nodded to the man standing near the front display. "That's a lovely hat," he said loudly enough for the man to hear. He turned to Chloe. "Our first customer of the day. I was hoping for more. We have so many new things to showcase." He stopped, serious for a moment, and then his eyes came alight. "How would you like a tour? We can pretend you're a customer. Perhaps a tycoon who's only in town for the night and looking for something spectacular. Perhaps the Queen herself! What say you?"

Chloe couldn't hide her excitement. "Yes please, Mr. Maddox! I would love that. Are you sure Mr. Ixworth won't mind?"

"Why would he mind?" said Maddox. "Also, you need to stop being so formal. You can call me Maddox. Ixworth is just Ixworth. No need for Mr.-Mr. It just seems so stuffy. We're all friends here."

Chloe blushed. She'd never thought a grownup would ever consider being her friend.

"Right, let's get started," said Maddox. "Come, come, there's so much to see."

Maddox took the tour seriously. It started immediately. "We keep our pens and bill of sale receipts in these," he said, pointing to an assortment of small drawers beneath the counter, each as deep as a teacup and wide enough to hold a stack of letters. Some of the drawers were marked with plaques of Egyptian bronze with rich Latin script while others were just left blank. Maddox then led her toward the doorway behind the counter. They stepped through into a narrow storeroom.

To the left, a sturdy rack braced the wall floor to ceiling. Shelves were packed with an assortment of oddities. Maddox pointed them out, explaining: candles that grew larger as they melted, self-fluffing pillows (both sides were the cool side), umbrellas that repelled the rain (and warmed those below their canopy), a 130-decibel bicycle horn, tweezers that pulled splinters on the first try, and a singing kettle that had a fondness for old nursery rhythms.

"These are ghost spectacles," said Maddox, placing the glasses on the top of his nose. "If I gifted you with a pair of these and you went outdoors, they'd allow you to see the paths of the departed. London's streets are alive with them."

"I think I'm okay without them," said Chloe with a shiver. "What's this?" she said, pointing to what looked like a small ski gondola that was standing in a corner beside the rack. Its roof was cream-coloured, and the bottom was bright red. It appeared to be just large enough to hold her and a good-sized suitcase.

"Oh yes!" said Maddox, clapping his hands together. "That's our *Spotter's Sky Taxi*. The first and only one of its kind." He opened the door so Chloe could see inside. The car was empty save a comfortable bench at the rear. There were no controls or levers, just a wide front window.

"What's it for?" said Chloe, immediately drawn to the cosy contraption.

"Simple," said Maddox, "you take a seat on the bench and the *Spotter's Sky Taxi* will take you anywhere you want to go, as long as you can see it through the forward window. A distant rooftop, the far side of a riverbank, a neighbour's balcony. Anything within sight."

"It can fly?" said Chloe.

"It's a Sky Taxi," shrugged Maddox. "When it moves, it's more of a putter. Quite slow. I wouldn't recommend sustained flight. Too many things could go wrong. One would really need to concentrate or risk plummeting to the ground. It's more for short journeys."

Chloe was breathless. "That doesn't sound possible," she said shyly. "I don't mean to sound mean, or rude, but ... how could something like that actually work? It doesn't have a propeller, and there's no wire attached to it."

"Why don't you try it?" said Maddox with a smirk.

"Wait. You mean here? Now?"

"Of course," said Maddox. He motioned for Chloe to climb in.

Chloe hesitated for only a moment, then before she even really knew what she was doing, she was inside the tiny box, seated on the comfortable bench, waiting for Maddox to tell her what to do next.

"To begin your journey," said Maddox, "look through the front window. See that self-sorting bookshelf in the opposite corner? Just tell the *Spotter's Sky Taxi* to take you there."

Chloe took a breath, wondering why she was so nervous. The trip was only the length of a room. She pointedly focused on the bookshelf. It was crafted from fine wood and stained nearly black. Leaves had been carved in the sideboards, climbing from the bottom to the top.

"Take me to the bookshelf, please," she said.

There was a peculiar noise—not a whir, for only common machines make whirring noises. This was more of a *wizzle*, then a *whirly-wump*, as the *Spotter's Sky Taxi* began to rise. Slowly, slowly, and when it was halfway between floor and ceiling, it began to slide forward through the air. Chloe giggled wildly, despite feeling silly for being so excited about such a tiny journey. When the *Spotter's Sky Taxi* finally settled at the foot of the bookcase and Chloe emerged from the cabin, her face hurt from smiling.

Maddox stood rooted to his spot, fists set firmly on his hips.

"Shall we continue our tour?" he said with a grin.

"You make all of this?" said Chloe, admiring the magical oddities around her.

"Of course," said Maddox. "We pride ourselves on offering only the highest quality merchandise. Useful items our customers may not realise they need until they see them in the flesh. It's the little touches that matter. That's why we're the finest curiosity shop in all of London."

"Ixworth said your shop is for other magicians," said Chloe, "so what's on display now?"

"We swap our merchandise at six o'clock sharp in readiness for our evening appointments," said Maddox. "Regular items move back here. Magical ones go out there."

Maddox pointed to a slender dining table. "I'm excited about this piece. It's one of our *crumb-less* tables. It absorbs spills and bits of food. No need to wipe the top. *Crumb-less.* Ixworth knows a man from Harrow with twenty-three grandchildren who's interested. We think it will fetch a good price."

Maddox brought them to the rear of the storeroom. On one side was an iron staircase that wound up to the second floor.

"These stairs lead to an office and a small flat," said Maddox. "My personal residence. Nothing too important. Just a desk and some files. I don't use it much. My living quarters are my own, although I have nothing to hide."

"What's that?" said Chloe, pointing to a large old-fashioned lift with pull doors that gleamed just to the left of the staircase.

"That's our lift," said Maddox. "Please be careful. It's old. Temperamental at times. I wouldn't want you getting hurt. I've pinched my fingers in the door mechanism more than once."

Chloe couldn't help staring at the old machine. "It only goes down?"

"We manufacture our curiosities in the basement workshop," said Maddox, nodding. "Our brownies bring them up when they're ready. I would love to show you, but they're hard at work, and I'd hate to disturb them."

"You have brownies working for you?" said Chloe.

"Yes indeed," said Maddox, "a busyness of brownies."

"I think they're a little scary," said Chloe.

"Oh, you have nothing to fear from brownies, m'dear," said Maddox.

"Where did they come from?"

Maddox shrugged. "Where does anybody come from? Salisbury, Grantham, Coventry ..."

"Do you pay them?" Chloe asked.

"Of course not," said Maddox. "Brownies have no need of money."

"Then why do they stay working for you?"

"Room and lodging, mostly," said Maddox. "We give them small gifts from time to time. The thing about brownies is they love their work through and through. They're doers! Meaning, they're not ones for lounging about eating grapes. They need to have a purpose. Give a brownie a purpose and he'll be as loyal as a duck."

Chloe finally turned away from the lift. "Have the brownies always worked for you, Maddox?"

Maddox shook his head. "Oh, the brownies aren't mine," he said, leading her back toward the front of the shop. "They're loyal to Ixworth. Essentially, they're his."

As Maddox exited to the front of the shop, Chloe allowed herself one last look at the magical oddities lined neatly along the shelves. They were as real as her own hand. Close enough that she could extend a finger and touch one. She could touch real magic. It was then and there Chloe decided Ixworth and Maddox's magical curiosity shop was the only place she wanted to be.

CHAPTER 4

OSWIN BLYTHE

A shop that employed a busyness of brownies took getting used to. Chloe had only seen them once, yet they were a nagging curiosity. Their presence could not be denied, for the work they completed in such a short time span was nothing short of miraculous. Each time Chloe arrived, she was treated to a new display of oddities the brownies had set up the night before, arranged with the most cunning care and attention to detail. Offerings of the highest quality and workmanship: a dark pine tea trolley with a colourful ceramic top; a tiny organ a quarter the size of any found in a church yet with a voice twice as loud; a richly carved oversized wardrobe with knobs in the shape of shaking hands; a device labelled "Cloud Juicer" ("If you're going to touch that, best open the door first," said Ixworth as Chloe peered at it). And these weren't even the magical items.

Ixworth and Maddox's shop was not busy. In those first days, only a few customers came in to have a look at the shop's offerings, but they rarely bought anything. Chloe hesitated to mention it; she thought it rude to ask how the two magicians hoped to make any money, but it seemed all the three of them ever did was sit and talk. Ixworth often asked about Chloe's schooling, for he had never gone himself. Maddox, on the other hand, was interested in Chloe's family. But he also liked to know about regular everyday things. "What's with those strange smiley face things people are always putting in places?" or "Does someone like me really need a phone plan?"

Chloe popped into the shop one Saturday about three weeks after she had learned of London's magical realms. Maddox was sitting behind the counter, reading from a folded slip of paper.

"Miss Chloe!" he cried, looking up. "I've been wondering what you've been getting up to all this week."

Chloe approached the counter, resting a hand on the smooth wood. "Just dumb stuff," she sighed. "Not as exciting as your week, I bet."

"To tell you the truth," said Maddox, "my week hasn't been all that interesting either. Although, my Cabot Cucumbers actually flowered for the first time."

"It must be nice to do whatever you want all the time," said Chloe. "I wish I didn't have to go to school."

"And why's that?" said Maddox, with a look of concern.

Chloe was hesitant to say more. There were a few kids in her grade who complained about everything: their favourite shows being cancelled or the boy they liked ignoring them. Piano lessons. Being allowed to invite only twenty people to their birthday parties. She didn't want to be one of those people. Yet Maddox actually seemed interested.

"I don't think I fit in very well," she said finally. "It sounds silly .... Sometimes I feel like everyone is noticing me too much or I have something on my nose and people are pointing at me or laughing behind my back. Lots of the time I just want to disappear."

"You have nothing on your nose," said Maddox saucily.

"You know what I mean," said Chloe.

Maddox watched her for a moment. "You know, it's hard being the age you are—how old are you again? Nineteen? Twenty?"

"Stoooop," said Chloe, trying her best not to smile.

"In all seriousness," Maddox said gently, "it's been a long while since I was your age. But I remember it. I had troubles like you. I often struggled with where I fit in or what I was to become, wondering if there was enough me to add up to anything important."

"Did it go away?" said Chloe.

"Well, yes and no," said Maddox. "Sometimes I still feel that way. Even now as a grown-up. But I'm wise enough to understand it's normal."

"I don't really feel all that normal," said Chloe.

"Who are these normal people you describe?" said Maddox. "There's no such thing as normal. Normal to one person is bonkers to another. I think you're perfect. Isn't that right, Ixworth?"

"What's this?" said Ixworth, who had just poked his head through the door from the rear of the shop.

"I was just musing on the qualities of wee Chloe. She has a queenly aura about her, wouldn't you say?"

Ixworth stepped out from behind the counter and looked at Chloe for a long moment. "She does have a certain way about her," he said cryptically. "Definitely wise beyond her years. I'll be off now. You two okay manning the shop?"

Maddox waved him away. "We're fine. Let's speak tomorrow. Say, did you read that article in the guild bulletin? About Mr. Brockwell?" Maddox held up the paper he had been reading. It was a newsletter. *The Quarterly Crow* was written in a banner across the top.

"He's disappeared."

"It came in the post this morning," said Ixworth, unfurling a paper from the inside of his tweed jacket. "I didn't have time to read it, so I brought it with me. Longer than usual, this one, yes?"

Maddox looked down at the one-sided newsletter in his hand. It was a brief communication of only three paragraphs. He shrugged.

"Let me know how things go," said Ixworth. He quickly departed, closing the shop door quietly behind him.

"Why is Ixworth leaving?" said Chloe. "Is he sick?"

"Heavens no," said Maddox. "I think he would call it, 'keeping the peace.' Ixworth is not a lover of conflict, as I'm sure you've guessed."

"Like, he's in a fight with someone?" said Chloe. "One of the people that came into the store today?"

Maddox shook his head. "Someone who booked one of our after-hours appointments. He ordered something special by request and is coming tonight to pick it up and look at some of our other offerings. I can't say I blame Ixworth for leaving, to tell you the truth."

"Oh?" said Chloe. "Ixworth hates someone so much he actually had to leave?"

"It's not so much that Ixworth dislikes him," Maddox said carefully, "more, this gentleman will do his best to annoy Ixworth if he knows he's here. Hence the return to his realm in Chelsea."

"Why would anyone want to annoy Ixworth?" said Chloe hotly. "He's so nice."

"I think that may be part of it," said Maddox. "Ixworth is such a level-headed man. I think that quality is bothersome to others, especially others who are of—*eh-hem*—of lesser character. Some of it has to do with the *Redistribution* of Kensington and Chelsea, I would imagine."

"You're going to have to explain, Maddox," said Chloe. "I have no idea what that means."

"I do apologise," said Maddox. "Sometimes I forget you're not one of us." He gave Chloe a wink. "Redistributed: broken apart into smaller portions. In the event of a magician's death, his or her realm can be awarded to another. Sometimes it's a person's son or daughter or a relative. Other times it's a stranger, just as long as the person receiving it is deemed a worthy enough magician. Byron Blythe lived in Kensington and Knightsbridge. When he died, his realm was split into two: One portion to his son, Oswin Blythe, who had spent half his lifetime lazily living in the shadow of his father and was deemed too young for the entire realm.

The other went to Cadence Ixworth, Ixworth's mother. Yet it wasn't to be: Cadence died of a mysterious illness shortly afterward and her realm was passed to Ixworth. Oswin was outraged."

Let me guess," said Chloe, "Oswin Blythe is coming here tonight?"

"Right you are," said Maddox.

"If you both don't like him so much, why do you let him come to your shop?"

Maddox sighed. "Politics, I'm afraid. Oswin Blythe has become a very influential magician. It would be unwise for us to be enemies. Better we all get along, or at least try to appear as though we get along."

"I don't like pretending to like people," said Chloe, "especially mean people."

"Well, Oswin Blythe fits that bill. Not a nice man by any means. Many of us loathe him. He's a boastful, greedy, disagreeable snot. Excuse my language. Some say he's undeserving of what he has. I would tend to agree.

"He sounds awful."

"Don't take my word for it," said Maddox, "you can judge for yourself if you like."

"How so?" said Chloe.

"He's coming at 4:00 pm. He insisted on an early appointment. Our regular hours weren't to his liking. Typical. Why don't you keep me company? I could use the support."

Maddox closed the shop a few minutes before three.

"I think the gloom has chased the shoppers anyway," he said as he removed the *open* sign from the window.

"But I suppose it's for the best. Blythe is going to demand our full attention. We wouldn't want any customers milling about after close."

"He's coming to look at the magical stuff?" said Chloe, remembering how fond she was of the *Spotter's Sky Taxi* and hoping it wasn't something Mr. Blythe would buy.

"Of course," replied Maddox. "Our magical oddities are the reason magicians come to us. Are you ready?"

"Ready for what?" said Chloe.

Maddox came around the counter to stand by the register. He opened one of the drawers beneath the countertop and removed a worn silver dinner bell. He gave it a quick shake, but it didn't make any noise. "Time to change the displays," he said.

A busyness of brownies hurried into the showroom from the rear of the shop. They were dressed in simple tunics of grey and cranberry red. Twelve in all. Tiny delicate beings with thin legs and knobbly knees, pointed beards and elf ears, who moved about jauntily, carting away the old display and replacing it with the new. They left four items: an ivory windowsill greenhouse, a writing desk three drawers high, a wooden document filing box, and a hat rack. It was the hat rack that took Chloe's breath away. It was heavyset, with thick legs that curved out and then in like the arms of an octopus. The trunk of the rack had been carved and bore the likeness of city streets. London streets: the College of Arms, the Library of Freemasonry, King's Cross, St. Paul's, winding and curving around the trunk from top to bottom.

In the briefest of moments, the brownies had come and gone.

"That was the craziest thing I've ever seen," said Chloe, grinning at the cleverness of the production.

Maddox smiled, pleased that Chloe was impressed. "They do have a way about them," he said. "We're blessed to have them in our service."

✦ ✦ ✦

There was a knock on the shop door at twenty past four. Maddox put down his book, *A Beginner's Guide to Making Romney Marsh Mash*, and went to answer. He drew the door back gracefully, allowing two men to enter.

"Good evening, gentlemen," he said with a flourish of his arm. "Welcome to *the Extraordinary Curiosities of Ixworth and Maddox*."

Chloe knew immediately which of the two men was Oswin Blythe, for she had never seen someone who carried such a snooty disposition. He was short, with thinning hair and a neat chin beard. He was richly dressed, even compared to the well-groomed Maddox, in a suit of such sheen that it seemed spun from metal. His sleeves were decorated with silver cufflinks. A ridiculous display of richness.

The man behind Mr. Blythe was like a giant block: nearly twice the size of Mr. Blythe with a tiny grape-shaped head perched on a stump-like neck. His massive upper trunk was slung with muscular arms, the short legs propped him up from beneath like an afterthought.

A bodyguard, thought Chloe. Clearly not a magician. His job description summarised in three words: I. Hurt. People.

"Take my coat," Mr. Blythe said to the Block.

The Block took the coat in his hand and bundled it neatly beneath his armpit. He assumed a guard-like pose.

"Good evening, Blythe," Maddox clucked.

"Maddox," said Mr. Blythe mildly.

Maddox extended his arm toward Chloe. "I'd like to introduce Miss Chloe, our ..." He paused, looking at Chloe. "Our—Ambassador of First Impressions and Customer Departures. She'll be assisting me with our showings."

Mr. Blythe gave Chloe a cold stare. "Does she check out?" he said sourly.

"She's one of us," said Maddox. "Tea?"

"Please," said Mr. Blythe.

"Right. I'll call for it now," said Maddox. He ambled behind the register, removed the little brownie bell from its drawer again and gave it a silent ring. "Feel free to have a look at our offerings," he said pointing to the front display, "I can answer your questions in a moment."

Maddox disappeared into the rear of the shop. To her horror, Chloe was left alone with the two men. She quickly opened a drawer below the countertop and pretended to look for something. It was safe to assume she wasn't supposed to talk to the other magicians.

Mr. Blythe moved toward the showings and gave them a brief look, but after a moment it became clear he was more interested in Chloe.

"You're not a magician, are you?" he said, slithering up to the counter.

"No," replied Chloe nervously.

"I guessed as much," said Mr. Blythe, examining her. "I think you'd be surprised."

"Surprised?" said Chloe.

"Many people are magicians—correction—could be magicians. They just don't know it."

"I don't want to be a magician," said Chloe.

Mr. Blythe smiled crookedly. "One needs talent to become a magician."

Chloe felt a sudden pang of pity for Ixworth. She had been in the presence of Oswin Blythe for only a moment and already understood what type of person he was.

"It's strange Ixworth and Maddox would allow you to hang around," Mr. Blythe continued. "You are aware this shop is different?"

"Yes," said Chloe trying her best to sound polite. "Ixworth and Maddox have shown me a lot of strange things."

Mr. Blythe looked thoughtful for a moment. "Do you live near here?" he said, returning his gaze to Chloe.

"Close," said Chloe.

"Not Kensington," said Mr. Blythe, as if he should know better. "I would sense it on you. Nothing goes on in my realm without me knowing about it."

The Block shifted his weight from one foot to the other, punctuating Mr. Blythe's last words.

"I live in Mayfair," said Chloe, channelling that

magical, if not practical, secret power women can conjure to mercilessly diminish boys. "Kensington is soooo drab. Plus, I like the shopping here much better."

Mr. Blythe stiffened. "Drab?"

Just then Maddox returned with a small troupe of brownies. They got to work setting a table in the corner near the register and laying it with a white tablecloth. Two of their number pulled a tea service piled with plates from the storeroom. Others brought food: spinach quiche with German mustard, mushroom puffs, a selection of finger sandwiches—cucumber, watercress and egg salad. There was a plate of baked goods: orange poppy seed loaf, strawberry ginger cake and scones with raspberry jam. Tea was served from a fine china pot.

"All friends now?" said Maddox pouring the tea.

Mr. Blythe nodded. "Your assistant is charming," he said icily. "Where did you find her?"

"You may not believe it," said Maddox, "but she just showed up unexpectedly at our front door." He handed Mr. Blythe a tidy cup and saucer painted with tiny blue flowers.

"I believe it," said Mr. Blythe.

Chloe smiled widely, which served to annoy Mr. Blythe even more.

"Tea for the large fellow?" said Maddox, motioning to the Block, who had barely moved since his arrival.

"He doesn't need anything," said Mr. Blythe dismissively. He gulped from his cup greedily. "Now, I've come here for a reason, Maddox, and that's not for chitchat. Tell me about these things you've set out for me."

Maddox took a sip of tea and placed his cup down gently in its saucer. He seemed used to Mr. Blythe's blunt manner.

"Right. We have three items this evening that may fit your needs."

"Only three?" said Blythe rudely. "What about my special request?"

Maddox smiled. "I didn't include that in the tally. Let us not forget, sometimes less is more."

Mr. Blythe drained his drink and put cup and saucer down hard on a corner of the front display.

"Let's hear about them then."

Maddox waved a hand toward the tidy windowsill greenhouse. "This was built to your specifications: deep, to accommodate tubers and roots, with a touch of StrangfordLough to provide the necessary tidal pull, an odd request, but … what is it they say? The customer is always right?" He returned to the counter, removing two sheets of paper and a writing pen from a drawer. Coming around, he approached the writing desk that stood at the front of the display.

"This artful piece is what we refer to as a Memory Desk," said Maddox. "Useful for those who, like me, are always jotting things down on paper and then forgetting where they've put them."

Maddox placed the papers on the desk. "Alas, so many lost poems."

He wrote his name on the paper in a curvy script.

When finished, he removed the paper from the desk and replaced it with the second blank sheet. He completed the ritual with three quick knocks on the desktop with the end of the pen. Immediately, the writing from the first sheet appeared on the second.

"Memory Desk."

The corners of Mr. Blythe's lips curled mischievously. Chloe imagined ways the man could misuse the creation. He could lure some unsuspecting person to the desk and have them scratch in a journal or sign a note. They would unknowingly reveal their darkest secrets. Personal, financial, or otherwise.

"Show me more," Mr. Blythe purred.

Maddox took Mr. Blythe's cup from the display, poured more tea and then handed it back in one fluid, practised motion. He returned to the display to pick up the small pine box. It was the length of a briefcase and perhaps three times as wide. The wood was worn, yet beautiful, with a rich carving of a tree on the lid.

"I have been told this is one of the most difficult things we've ever made," said Maddox, looking down at the box in his hands. "It kept coming apart all of its own. Fortunately, we had some rare blessed wood on hand which managed to bind it properly."

Both Mr. Blythe and Chloe peered at the box, but its purpose was unclear. Maddox opened the lid, yet it still remained a mystery. Even the Block moved closer to take a look.

"What is it?" said Mr. Blythe, staring at it.

"We call it a *Wherebox*," said Maddox.

"A what?" said Mr. Blythe.

"A *Wherebox*."

"Made up words?" said Mr. Blythe. " I've never heard of a *Wherebox*."

"Well, it had to be called something," said Maddox.

"Its purpose?" said Mr. Blythe.

"Whatever is placed in the box disappears."

Mr. Blythe yawned rudely. "Disappears? Now there's a new trick. Honestly, Maddox. You're wasting my time."

Maddox was prepared for this. "Let's not get ahead of ourselves," he explained. "In essence, a *Wherebox* is the safest of safe boxes. An object placed inside is gone. Truly gone. A *Fetch* will not retrieve it. A *Wide-Eye* cannot see it. Even those blessed with clairvoyance will be unaware of it. Place something in a *Wherebox* and it disappears. From the world."

Mr. Blythe looked at the *Wherebox* thoughtfully. "It's immune to spells?"

"Through and through," said Maddox.

"And strong?" said Mr. Blythe.

"It was constructed from seven separately blessed woods. Two planks from the grove at Thames Head in Gloucestershire, two boards from Birnam Wood, a bough of Methuselah bristlecone pine, and two boards fashioned from Niagara white cedar. Each was cured for 953 days and blessed with seven drops of *Krubera Water*. It's very strong."

It took a moment for Mr. Blythe to come to terms with this new information, but then sensing a need for such a thing, he said: "Interesting."

Mr. Blythe took a step closer to Maddox letting his hand hover above the worn wood without touching it. "What's inside is completely gone. Completely?"

Maddox smiled. "I reckon the greatest magician in London would have a hard time seeing the box, let alone discovering its contents."

Mr. Blythe's eyes grew wide. "What a marvellous contraption," he said greasily. "Very practical. Tell me Maddox, which one of you dreamt up and had the patience to create this little darling?"

Maddox smiled. "I wish it were me," he said. "Alas, Ixworth is the mastermind behind today's showings."

Mr. Blythe's smile grew wicked. "Yes. Ixworth. I like that old boy. Where is he this evening? The two of you seem to have a good thing going here. I'd like to congratulate him in person if I could."

Maddox placed the Wherebox near the front of the display. "Ixworth had some errands to run, unfortunately. But he sends his regards."

Mr. Blythe had trouble hiding his disappointment. "Of course. Well … perhaps I'll ring again soon. Thank him myself."

"Very well," said Maddox, moving toward the last of the featured furnishings. "Would you like to know about this last one? Come closer and examine the artistry."

Mr. Blythe stepped forward. "It's splendid," he said, "but I don't need to look it over."

"Oh. Are you sure?" said Maddox, looking disappointed. "Ixworth says it's tuned to the weather, will swivel the proper garment to the front depending on the day—"

"I'm quite sure," said Mr. Blythe.

"Just the desk and the *Wherebox,* then?" said Maddox.

"No," said Mr. Blythe.

Maddox sighed. "A shame. I'm sorry we couldn't be more helpful today. Perhaps we can schedule another appointment soon. We may have something more to your liking then."

"Nonsense," said Mr. Blythe. "I'll be taking the lot!"

"Oh!" said Maddox, looking pleased. "I'll arrange to have them delivered."

"Do as you must," said Mr. Blythe. "You have my address." He drained his cup.

The Block, accustomed to the abruptness of his master, handed him his coat.

"One last thing," said Mr. Blythe.

"Of course," said Maddox.

"Your assistant ..."

"Chloe."

"Right. I should like it if she weren't here next time."

"Oh?" said Maddox.

"She's a little too common for my liking. Have her do something else. Something away from the shop. Maybe she can help Ixworth run his ... errands."

Turning, Mr. Blythe and the Block departed brashly, like the door to the shop was an annoyance and the pavement beyond something that needed to be trodden upon with heavy boots.

CHAPTER 5

CRUMMOCK WATER

Dad was complaining about the heat for the third day in a row. It had been an unusually hot May, and the home air conditioner, which had never worked properly to Chloe's knowledge, was blowing warm air instead of cool.

"You would think after paying for something to get fixed, it would stay fixed," said Dad, red faced after huffing up the stairs. Chloe, who normally didn't mind summer weather, agreed. A nice trip to the sea was in order.

The shop was different and otherworldly when Chloe arrived that weekend. There were leaves covering the wall behind the stage, spreading upward and outward across the ceiling like a lush forest canopy. A gentle breeze, perhaps urged indoors from some hidden London wood, shook them gently. It left Chloe with the odd sensation of standing in a space much larger than it actually was.

"When did you do all this, Ixworth?" said Chloe, unable to tear her eyes from the ceiling.

Ixworth was fussing with a stack of board games:

The Angry Ottoman; Escape from Filther's Gulch; Mr. Butterbrow's Briar.

"Do all what?"

"You've brought a forest into the shop. Or haven't you noticed?"

"Oh, just a little thing I cooked up," said Ixworth. "It's a tad hot. I thought it might be a treat for us and our customers."

"Well, this is a relief," said Chloe. "Our air conditioner is broken. The house feels like an oven."

Ixworth seemed sympathetic yet slightly confused by the concept of air conditioning. Then he suddenly perked up.

"I've brought you something," he said.

"Oh?" said Chloe, who loved surprises.

Ixworth left the front display to retrieve something from behind the register. He returned, standing beside Chloe, a worn lavender baking tin in his hands. He popped the lid. Inside were a half dozen jackets of apple strudel dusted in fine cinnamon. "Try one," he said.

Chloe took one of the delicate bundles. The pastry had been flogged and kneaded so thin the layers were nearly transparent. She took a bite. And then, despite her good manners, another and then another.

"These. Are. So. Good," she said. "Did one of your busyness bake them?"

Ixworth smiled shyly as he watched Chloe lick her fingers. "These were made with my own hands. No magic. It's my mother's recipe. She taught me years ago. Mother was a trained pastry chef. She learned from some of the finest teachers on the continent." Ixworth offered the container again, and Chloe took another strudel. "It's a pity you couldn't have met her. I think she would have liked you very much."

He returned to the counter, and for a moment, Chloe thought he looked sad.

"I don't make these that often," he said after a moment. "But I like to leave them for Maddox. He could do with a little more meat on him."

"Is Maddox out today?" said Chloe, suddenly aware of the calmness of the shop without their chattier companion.

"He had business elsewhere," said Ixworth. "Probably out shopping for rare herbs. Speaking of business, Maddox mentioned you met Oswin Blythe."

"Yes. Him," said Chloe, scrunching her face as if Oswin Blythe were the name of an unpleasant odour that had suddenly shot up her nose. "He was a little ... I'm not sure how to say it. I can only think of bad words."

Ixworth, never one for strong displays of emotion, chuckled quietly. "Mr. Blythe is an interesting fellow. I'm not sure what Maddox told you."

"Not much," said Chloe. "Just that he didn't like you very much. He thought it wasn't right that you inherited your family's realm. Why wouldn't you? It belonged to your mother."

Ixworth shrugged. "I suppose he thought it unfair, considering I already had a small realm. There are those who are never satisfied with what they have and always want more." Ixworth sighed. He turned to give one last satisfied look to the front window display. "I guess I should open the shop, no?"

Chloe hung about for much of the day while Ixworth puttered about. The shop had a wonderful way of putting her at ease. When she was there, all of the messiness with school and being an eleven-year-old didn't seem to matter.

When Chloe announced it was time for her to go, Ixworth met her at the door.

"Here," he said, handing her a wide-mouth mason jar labelled *Crummock Water*. "Try this."

"What is it?" asked Chloe, examining the clear liquid inside.

"Think pond in a bottle," said Ixworth. "In your case, a way to keep cool. Best kept a secret. Something to do when your parents aren't about."

"I still don't understand," said Chloe.

"All you need to do," Ixworth explained, "is pour this out. Lawn and green grass work best. If you have a yard, that will do nicely. Be precise and concise, as *Crummock Water* has a mind of its own. When you release the water, you'll need to shape it. Tell it what it needs to be. For example: A fresh pond, not deep, two yards by three yards, no swell, lake temperature. You can cool off and swim when it's hot. When you're finished, drop the mason jar into the pond, and it will collect itself."

Chloe held the jar like it was the most precious thing on earth. "How-how-how?" she stammered.

"Never you mind," said Ixworth. He pulled

something from his jacket pocket. "Here, wrap it in this handkerchief. I haven't used it, don't worry. It will save the bottle breaking when you're transporting it. Do you have your rucksack?"

* * *

The hot weather continued, and Chloe was desperate to try the *Crummock Water*. It was less as a matter of cooling down, more because she was actually carrying around magic in a bottle. When she came down for breakfast Sunday morning, she hoped to find the kitchen empty. The piles of discarded newspapers beneath the kitchen table and the smell of burnt toast indicated Dad had been there but was now gone. But where was Mum? The sound of the push mower whirred in from the open window. She made toast, making sure to butter the edges of the bread, and then dolloped a heavy spoonful of jam in the middle like it was a poached egg. She carried her plate to the garden.

The Ashleys' yard was small: a few loosely placed patio stones and some scattered lilacs and fruit trees around a small patch of lawn. A grate in the back corner caught the runoff from the surrounding houses. Chloe had been scared of going near it when she was younger. It made odd sloshing sounds after it rained, and she had nightmares about monsters crawling out from below and coming into the house.

Mum was leaning on the push mower and talking loudly on her mobile, something about "resale values," "amenities," and "curb appeal." She gave Chloe a distracted wave.

Chloe took a seat on the lawn, chewing her crusts. Mum finally hung up. She leant the mower against the house beside the drainpipe and then made a quick inspection of one of the garden's pear trees.

"Ugh," she said. "I'm about to give up on this."

"What's wrong with your tree?" said Chloe.

Mum kneaded some of the young leaves between her fingers. "It doesn't like me," she said. Her mobile rang. Mum held a shushing finger. "One sec, Chlo."

Chloe collected her plate and moved back toward the house. Why were regular grown-ups so boring?

The *Crummock Water* would have to wait.

✦ ✦ ✦

"How does one become a magician?" Chloe asked Maddox one Saturday in early June. She had been hanging about the shop for over a month, and it was beginning to feel like a second home.

"I had a mentor of course," said Maddox, cutting the stems from a bunch of dried marigolds and placing the petals into a small manilla envelope.

"Let me guess," said Chloe, "a gardener—or, wait. Someone who sells flowers."

"A florist?" said Maddox.

"Yeh," said Chloe. "I thought you needed to know about plants to become a magician?"

Maddox smiled. "Not true. Look at Ixworth. He

doesn't know a thing about plants. Why else would his elixirs and tonics be so terrible?"

"I never knew they were," said Chloe.

"Ixworth couldn't concoct an elixir if he were in the dead centre of his kingdom on a full moon," said Maddox. "However, his *Paroxysm* has always been spot-on. His *Flexure* is one of the finest I've ever seen."

"His what?"

"*Flexure*."

"What's that?"

"Tut-tut," said Maddox, "if you're going to associate with magicians, you really need to start catching on."

"Catching on?" said Chloe. "Like, learn about magic?"

"Might be a good idea to learn some of our language at the very least," said Maddox.

"Can normal people become magicians?" asked Chloe. "Someone like me?"

"Of course," said Maddox. "I used to be someone just like you. How do you think I became a magician?"

"I thought maybe people were just born with magic."

"Oh, heavens no," said Maddox. 'I've never heard of that happening, at least amongst the London magicians. It's possible, I suppose, but not very likely."

"So your mum and dad weren't magicians?" said Chloe, watching Maddox carefully seal the manilla envelope with a bit of damp sponge.

"I never knew my father for more than a moment," replied Maddox. "And my mother ... well, she was kind, but practical. She wouldn't have made a good magician."

"So this mentor. He taught you magic? But he wasn't a florist?"

"My mentor didn't have a trade," said Maddox. "Unless 'scoundrel' counts as a trade. But let's not talk about that."

Chloe watched Maddox file the envelope in one of the drawers beneath the counter.

"Will you teach me a trick?" she said after a moment.

"What kind of a trick?" said Maddox.

"I'm not sure. What's this *Flexure* thing you were talking about?"

Maddox coughed politely. "A *Flexure* is a difficult thing even for the best of us, m'dear."

"What is it?" asked Chloe.

"A way of moving from place to place."

"Disappearing?"

"Not exactly. More folding and unfolding. A *Flexure* requires some very specific and precise magic. A thorough understanding of where you are and where you need to end up. It's not something one decides to conjure on a whim. It's very serious stuff. I once knew of a young magician who thought he knew his realm well enough to try and fold the corners of Limeburner Lane and Ludgate Hill and ended up putting half of himself in St. Paul's Churchyard and the other on the banks of the Thames."

"You're serious?" said Chloe.

"Absolutely."

"Isn't it the same thing as teleporting?"

Maddox scoffed. "Breaking apart atoms and

recreating them elsewhere? Teleportation is impossible."

Chloe raised an eyebrow. "But almost the same?"

"There are subtle differences."

"Okay, sorry," said Chloe. "So if Ixworth's Flixy—"

"*Flexure.*"

"—if *Flexure* is so good, why doesn't he use it all the time? Can't he just pop into the shop from his house?"

"If only it were that easy," said Maddox. "Like all spells, a *Flexure* has its drawbacks. It requires a great deal of preparation. One must be careful when using it. Some magicians put up obstacles to stop that sort of thing."

"Obstacles?" said Chloe.

"Counter spells," said Maddox, "to stop other magicians from arriving unexpectedly in one's realm. We hate that sort of thing."

A small voice suddenly called from the storeroom, "Mr. Maddox, are you there?"

Maddox clapped his hands. "This way," he called back. Turning to Chloe, he said, "I want to introduce you to somebody."

"Oh?" said Chloe.

"Yes, yes, yes," said Maddox, "Mr. Winch."

Chloe leaned against the counter. "Who?"

"Mr. Winch, here," said Maddox. "Who did you think?"

Maddox looked down, recognizing the problem. "Winch, come out from there so Chloe can have a look at you."

The gentleman in question, Mr. Winch, came

around the counter. To Chloe's great surprise, he was a brownie. He was dressed in a trim brown suit of wool, a red bow tie and pointed black shoes with the laces tied in neat double knots. His beard was small and patchy. A young brownie.

"Very pleased to meet you, Miss," said Mr. Winch in a clear voice. He held out a tiny brownie hand toward Chloe.

Chloe took his hand cautiously. The palm was warm, the skin soft, a surprise given brownies' love of hard work. She suddenly realised she was shaking the hand of something she had once thought imaginary.

"Chloe. You can stop shaking Winch's hand now," said Maddox.

"Right. Of course," said Chloe. "Sorry."

"It's no trouble at all," said Mr. Winch kindly, looking at Chloe. "You have a nice way about you."

"Do you work here, Mr. Winch?" Chloe asked.

"Yes," said the brownie, "Mr. Ixworth and Mr. Maddox have been kind enough to hire me," he said proudly.

"That's right," added Maddox. "With sales starting to pick up, Winch can help me with some of my special projects."

"Oh?" said Chloe, who suddenly wondered why Maddox wouldn't ask the busyness they already employed to help. "Nice to meet you, Mr. Winch."

"You and Winch will become great friends, I'm sure," said Maddox. "He'll be operating behind the scenes during the day. I'm very excited to have him join us."

Mr. Winch blushed. Turning, he addressed Chloe: "My father has known Mr. Maddox for one hundred and thirty-five years and once worked for him. It's an honour for me, my father and my family to have the opportunity to offer my services."

"We're glad to have you," said Maddox, putting a hand on Mr. Winch's small shoulder. "Now come, let's get you settled."

Mr. Winch bowed low. "So nice to have met you, Chloe," he said before nipping off behind Maddox toward the rear of the shop.

* * *

Chloe's walk home from the curiosity shop was sunlit and summery. Ahead, the streets were flooded with a rich gold light, giving them a carnival's air. Around her, happy couples and small groups were walking, making their way to restaurants or nightly events. Chloe felt suddenly resentful. She had no mates to be heading off somewhere with.

Alone with her thoughts, she carried on. At Binney Street, she noticed a man watching her from the opposite side of Weighhouse Street. He was old, perhaps in his sixties, with long slicked-back hair. He wore a grey suit with a tattered scarf about his shoulders, giving him a grimy look. He was leaning against a lamp post, but as Chloe approached, he straightened and took a step closer to the street. As she passed, the man smiled wickedly. Chloe was filled with an inexplicable feeling of terror.

Mum and Dad had given Chloe the appropriate talk about the dangers of London streets. She turned quickly, marching north toward the bustle of Oxford Street. The man followed slowly, crossing Binney, his gaze deliberate, eyes never from her.

Chloe turned the corner onto the high street, her rucksack jostling into people as she back-tracked east. Reaching Gilbert Street, she paused for a moment, wondering if her imagination was getting the better of her, but the man appeared, spotting her at the corner.

Chloe ran south on Gilbert. There was a private park halfway down the block. An iron gate enclosed the space, but a landscaper who was stowing his tools in a nearby lorry had left it open. With no other option, Chloe slipped through the gate and crouched behind a small shrub. She had a sudden thought.

Chloe struggled out of her rucksack and unzipped the top. Frantically she removed the *Crummock Water* from its nest beneath her school sweater. She unwrapped the handkerchief and unscrewed the lid. Ixworth had said to be specific. She poured the *Crummock Water* on a small patch of grass near her feet. "Small pond. Waist deep. No swell. Lots of reeds. Mist."

Chloe had never seen a spell at work. She had imagined a pond would appear instantly when she poured out the *Crummock Water*. Yet it was less a transformation and more a washing away of the old. It was as if the small patch of grass in the private garden had never existed. Grass? A park? In this spot? It seemed such a silly notion. But this tiny kidney-shaped pond of murky water, enclosed in a wall of brooding bulrushes and cattails, surely had always been there.

With little time for deliberation, Chloe leapt in, clothes and all. She gasped when she hit the water, for it was frigid. If she hadn't been in such a hurry, she would have made the water warmer. Less boggy too. But there was no time to worry about that. Stealthily she crept among the mist-tipped reeds, parting them slightly as she scanned the street.

Chloe saw the man pass once, then again, the wiry scarecrow-like figure unmistakable. She crouched in the chilly water until her legs were numb and teeth were chattering. When she couldn't stand it any longer she crept cautiously to the bank, being careful not to disturb the rushes. After a few breaths, she snuck up to the iron fence and dared a look to the street. Gilbert Street was empty, save a woman making a delivery on the opposite side. Chloe returned to the pond and removed the *Crummock* jar from her backpack. When the jar touched the water, the pond collected itself, disappearing much like it had appeared. The tiny green space returned to normal.

Chloe retreated soggily to Oxford Street, ignoring the wide-eyed stares of shoppers. When she felt it was safe, she ran west until her chest burned. Reaching Park Street, she dared one terrified look over her shoulder before turning south again toward home. To her relief, the man was nowhere to be seen.

CHAPTER 6

THE VALEN'S ENCHANTMENT

Ixworth never asked Chloe about the *Crummock Water*. For all intents and purposes, the subject was forgotten. He wasn't one for chatting endlessly about a topic. They had talked about the *Crummock Water*. He had given it to Chloe. That was that. A part of her wished he would ask. She wanted to tell him about the frightening man who'd followed her. Yet she wondered if it was her place to burden him with her silly fears. Ixworth wasn't one of her parents. If it had been Maddox who'd given her the *Crummock Water*, things might have been different. He couldn't stop himself from talking about something shared, as Chloe was about to find out.

"I've decided something," said Maddox the following Sunday.

"You have?" said Chloe, who had just checked her mobile and was wondering why she hadn't any messages. She and Iris had made up, but they talked less and less, and she was starting to fear her only close friend had forgotten her.

"I was thinking I could teach you a thing or two about magic," said Maddox.

"You will?" said Chloe, eyes alight, heart fluttering. Using the *Crummock Water* had sparked a fire. It was one thing to see magic at work, but to actually handle it—pour it out of a jar and use it herself—that was thrilling.

"Yes," said Maddox. "It will be our secret. Won't Ixworth be surprised when he realises we have another accomplished magician working in our little shop?"

"What kind of things will you teach me?" said Chloe excitedly.

Maddox scratched at his beard. "Something small enough that if you practise hard you just might get the hang of it before the end of the summer. Keep in mind, you have no realm to call your own, so your growth will be limited."

"That long?" said Chloe frowning.

Maddox raised an eyebrow. "This isn't a recipe for custard, Miss Chloe. Magic is hard work."

"I'm sorry, Maddox," said Chloe. "I'm just a little excited. I understand. What do I need to do?"

"Read this," said Maddox, removing a small worn notebook from his jacket pocket. He placed it on the counter beside the register. "I've written a few notes for you. You should look them over—after you've finished any schoolwork, of course."

Maddox withdrew his attention, intent on sorting a drawer full of old filings. Chloe desperately wanted the notebook but didn't want to appear too eager. It felt impolite. It sat like a bright red sweet, nagging for attention for the next hour. When a customer placed their hand on it while paying for something at the register, Chloe gave in, sweeping it away quietly to the safety of her rucksack.

After the shop closed, Chloe hurried home. She tore through dinner with barely a word, which unsurprisingly, went unnoticed, as Mum and Dad were arguing over which colour to paint the kitchen. After helping clear the dishes, Chloe crept to her room, heart pounding, wondering if it were truly possible to learn magic by reading a few instructions.

Chloe removed the notebook from her rucksack: the pages were bound in worn cloth, the paper thick and speckled like the book had been made by hand. Maddox had written on the first blank page, his handwriting unmistakable, the ink strokes long and elegant.

It said:

THE *VALEN'S ENCHANTMENT*

1. Each hand: pinch thumb and index finger. Place formed fingers together, facing inward, forming a small space. A *Rosebud*.
2. Turn formed fingers: clockwise with left hand, counterclockwise with right. A motion similar to popping a cap from a bottle of cordial. My favourite is lemon, although the lime is quite good too.
3. The *Rosebud* should stay put, despite one's instinct to think it has changed with the

movement of your fingers. Retain the shape in your mind. Remember it! It will hold together if you concentrate. You're simply bending it. This is tricky.

4. When you have successfully trapped the *Rosebud,* pinch thumb and index fingers tightly, and slowly pull them apart. Like you were pulling apart warm toffee.

Chloe read through Maddox's instructions several times. It seemed an easy exercise, yet the details were vague. The first part was straightforward enough: pinch thumb and forefinger together. No bother.

Next, Chloe rotated her formed, pinched fingers, but stopped when she had to check which direction to turn each hand. Clockwise: Left. Counterclockwise: Right.

Chloe understood the idea of the *Rosebud* for the third step yet didn't understand how to keep the space from smushing between her fingers. She tried. Failed. Tried again. Gave up, and then decided to move to the final step.

Chloe imagined a spider's web tying her hands together. This seemed more fitting than Maddox's comparison to warm toffee. Typical of Maddox to be thinking about food. It was a miracle he didn't weigh a hundred stone. Slowly Chloe pulled her fingers apart.

Nothing happened.

Chloe crumpled her fingers together and then made a motion like throwing away a wadded-up paper. It seemed conjuring magic was more difficult than pouring water from a jar and giving a few commands. She would have to think about this. The *Valen's Enchantment* was going to take practice.

✦ ✦ ✦

Maddox was right about the shop's evening appointments really picking up. One night, a young magician from Stoke Newington purchased five items for himself and two others as gifts for his relatives. The rest of the week's showings were all full, and the shop was double-booked for Friday. Yet the days were still slow, the customers infrequent. Ixworth, Maddox, and Chloe had a lot of spare time, and reading seemed the perfect diversion, especially for the shop's quieter inhabitants.

After discovering Chloe was a fan of reading, Ixworth began to bring books for her. Magician stories: *The Darkening of Nicholas Mallow*; *Grod of Grange*; *The Gentle Herd of Farmer Soum from Woodbastion*; and *Crawswale Smeek*, the tale of a legendary magician who attempted to sail from Falmouth to Vila Do Corvo and found himself in a dead calm for a month. Chloe and Ixworth had taken to reading, the two of them, on afternoons when business was slow. Out of all the miraculous things Chloe had experienced since starting at the curiosity shop, these lazy afternoons had become her favourite.

"Have you ever read this?" said Ixworth, handing

Chloe a copy of *Twill and the Fields of Billow* shortly after Chloe arrived on Wednesday.

"Of course not," said Chloe smiling. "I've never heard of any of your books." Chloe took the dusty volume from Ixworth. She enjoyed the magician stories. They were darker and more grown-up than anything she had read. She liked the honesty of the writing: sometimes good things happened to the characters. Sometimes not.

Chloe and Ixworth were interrupted when the shop door suddenly opened. A hulking figure entered. Chloe recognized him immediately as Mr. Blythe's bodyguard, the Block. He had to have eaten recently (a whole cow?), for he seemed larger than Chloe remembered.

"Can I help you?" said Ixworth.

"I'm looking for Mr. Blythe," said the Block with a voice that sounded like loose gravel rattling inside a dryer.

"I'm afraid he's not here," said Ixworth.

The man glared at them suspiciously. "When did you see him last?"

Ixworth shrugged. "He was in the shop some time ago. I assume he was with you."

"You sure?" said the Block.

"Well, I'm sure," said Ixworth. "Are you?"

"Mind if I have a look around?" said the Block.

"You can have a look at our offerings," said Ixworth.

"What's back there?" said the Block, pointing toward the rear of the shop.

"That's our store room," said Ixworth.

"I'd like a quick look," said the Block.

"Private, I'm afraid," said Ixworth.

"Just quick."

Chloe was getting nervous. The Block's arm must have been the same width as Ixworth's waist.

"Employees only," said Ixworth calmly.

"You two going to stop me?" said the Block, looking at Ixworth and then Chloe.

"I'm okay with him having a look if you are," said Chloe to Ixworth.

The Block moved toward the storeroom.

"That's far enough," said Ixworth, coming around the counter.

The Block's massive body tensed. He took a step closer to Ixworth. Violence seemed unavoidable.

"Have a bit of *Pickled Redherring*," said Ixworth.

"A bit of what?" the Block said stupidly.

"*Pickled Redherring*."

Chloe had difficulty following what happened next. Ixworth made an elaborate motion with his hand, a ring circus of twirling fingers. A moment later, the Block was staggering backward. It took a moment for the giant man to regain his balance, but when he stood back up, his face was awash in confusion.

"What have you done to him?" said Chloe, noting the Block's dazed look. She stepped out from the safety of the counter. "Have you killed him?"

"Of course not," said Ixworth, taking a moment to examine his handiwork. "It's *Pickled Redherring*. Harmless. I'll instruct him once he's settled down."

"Instruct him?" said Chloe.

"Yes," said Ixworth. "I'm tempted to send him on a long walk to Brighton, but that would be unkind. I'll send him home instead."

Chloe approached the Block. She resisted the urge to poke the massive man. "*Pickled Redherring*: hypnotising, yes?"

"In a sense," nodded Ixworth. "More a befuddling of one's immediate thoughts. Unlike a hypnotism, he'll remember this."

Ixworth moved closer to the Block and spoke directly to him like he was talking long distance to someone on the telephone. "Won't. You. Sir?"

Chloe stifled the urge to giggle. She had never witnessed such a reversal of power. "What's next?"

Ixworth moved closer to the Block and looked into his small black eyes. "Now, hear this," he announced. "I'm not sure what Mr. Blythe taught you about magicians—or manners—but you don't go marching into someone's shop and start making demands."

Chloe watched Block's face. If he could hear what Ixworth was saying, he didn't respond. Yet he must have understood something, for there were large beads of moisture on his forehead.

"I'll get to the point," said Ixworth, addressing the Block as if he were a child. "You need to go home now, wherever that is. Don't hurt yourself on the way. Have Mr. Blythe get in touch, by telephone preferably. My partner and I will let him know about your rude behaviour. I doubt he'll be disappointed. He probably put you up to it."

The Block flinched as if someone had slapped him with something slimy and grotesque.

"Now go!" Ixworth commanded.

It was Chloe's turn to flinch. There was power in Ixworth's words. One not paying attention might have done Ixworth's bidding even without the *Pickled Redherring*. Chloe put a hand on the countertop to steady herself.

The Block instantly complied. He came out of his trance, took one cowering look at Ixworth, and rushed out the door.

"Where does Blythe hire his help?" said Ixworth after the shop door had closed. "Bullies working for bullies."

"That was really weird," said Chloe.

"I agree," said Ixworth. "You would think this would be the last place anyone would come looking for Blythe."

"Mr. Blythe doesn't seem like a man who would do anything by himself," said Chloe.

"You're right about that," said Ixworth. He looked thoughtful.

"What is it?" said Chloe.

"I don't know," said Ixworth. "I wonder if Blythe is up to something. Like you said, he doesn't go anywhere without his entourage."

"Entourage?" said Chloe.

"A group of followers. Bodyguards, assistants. People paid to do his bidding."

"I know this sounds bad," said Chloe, watching the door, "but if something happened to him, I wouldn't be surprised. Blythe is such a mean man. At least he was when I met him."

Ixworth thought for a moment. "Mr. Blythe is very influential. It would be unwise to openly challenge him," he said.

"But why else would someone disappear without telling his bodyguard where he was going?"

Ixworth shrugged. "A good question," he said. "Honestly, I haven't a clue."

CHAPTER 7

THE DISAPPEARANCE OF MR. IXWORTH

Chloe set Maddox's notebook on her bedside table. She was tired of reviewing the *Valen's Enchantment*. She had been obsessing over the simple instructions since Maddox had given them to her. But the excitement of learning real magic was gone. It had become homework. For Chloe, the idea of placing a spell inside a *Rosebud* seemed ridiculous. What did it mean? How could one put something inside of nothing? The instructions, *Pinch thumb and forefinger, hands clockwise, counterclockwise, spiderweb fingers,* seemed simple enough, but in reality it was as difficult as anything she had ever tried. Chloe had discovered, much like her attempts the week before, that the most troublesome part of the *Rosebud* (which should have been called a contortion of messy finger movements) was the final step: the retention. It was just so hard to hold something imaginary.

Huddled in her room that Saturday, Chloe gave up, a decision that brought resentment and relief in equal measure. Saddened, she picked up the notebook, suddenly tempted to throw it, send it flapping across the room to punish it for all of the wasted hours. But she couldn't do that. Maddox had taken the time to write down the instructions. He had trusted her with so much. He deserved better.

Chloe put the book down and lay on her bed, staring at the ceiling. Her mobile sat idle nearby. She was frustrated and wanted to talk to someone, but everyone she knew seemed ordinary and uninteresting. She got up and moved to the window as a gloomy cloud crossed the sun, paling the light. She shivered in the sudden seemingly unnatural shade.

✦ ✦ ✦

On Sunday, the *Rosebud* was top-of-mind for Maddox. Chloe was afraid to tell him of her troubles so decided to just play along.

"Once you have a *Rosebud*, you'll need to pop a piece of magic in it," said Maddox.

"And how do I do that?" said Chloe.

Maddox touched his temple with his index finger. "It's all up here, m'dear."

"That's not going to help me very much," said Chloe flatly.

Maddox thought for a moment. "I'll put it like this: the *Valen's Enchantment* is a gesture that *asks*—politely of course—for something to change its state."

"I really wish I knew what that meant," said Chloe,

doing her best to sound interested. Talking about it was making her irritable.

"Let me try and think of an example," said Maddox, pacing in front of the register. "Right. I often use the *Valen's Enchantment* when I garden. I entice my flowers, well, herbs mostly, to grow quickly. In a sense, I'm asking them to change."

"You ask your flowers to change?" said Chloe. "How?"

"It's not so much the asking, more envisioning," said Maddox. "Not just the beginning and end results, but all of the stages in between. The rest of the enchantment involves *baking*."

Chloe sighed heavily. "Maddox, you're making it hard to keep track of all this."

Maddox paused for a moment. "My apologies," he said finally. "I am, of course, speaking in metaphor for the sake of explanation. I'm talking about steps and processes. Baking is another word for precision. One prepares a spell like a chef would prepare a recipe. Step one leads to step two. Step three after step two and so-forth. To make a successful enchantment, one must follow the steps, no matter how one goes about it. All magicians prepare differently. Some envision a painting: they, the artist, paint the enchantment. Each brush stroke is one step. Others magicians craft: every move a board of wood, a brick, a stitch of thread."

Chloe thought about this, and for a brief moment, understood. "I think I follow."

"Fantastic," said Maddox. "Now, after one *bakes*, the

next step involves the *Realisation* of the end result."

"You need to give more examples," said Chloe. "You're using a lot of words that mean more than one thing."

Maddox straightened like an actor about to say his line. "Right. An example could be, 'Goodness, my ivy has grown seven feet in just a day. The roots themselves must weigh at least twelve stone.'"

"That's the *Realisation?*" said Chloe. "And after that?"

"A polite, and cordial *pleading* never hurts. A lesson to be had in life, I might add. I top off all my enchantments with a sprinkle of *hope*."

"Hope?"

"To the order of, 'I really hope this works out for the best,'" said Maddox.

"You just made that up," said Chloe, smiling despite her best efforts to stay grumpy.

Just then Ixworth hurried in through the front of the shop, banging the door loudly.

"I thought you weren't coming in today?" said Maddox, turning to look at him.

Ixworth didn't answer right away. He held something in his hand: a slip of paper that he kept unfolding and refolding. He looked at Chloe and Maddox nervously. "I wasn't?"

"You said you had some things to do around the house," said Maddox. "Remember?"

"Oh, right. That," said Ixworth. "That's all taken care of. I guess I forgot to tell you." He stood rooted to the spot until several customers entered the shop behind him. Startled, Ixworth moved away from the door, sliding toward the register as a family of tourists sporting *I survived the London Underground* t-shirts filed in. Maddox came around the counter to greet them. Ixworth exited to the rear of the shop.

After a moment, Chloe followed Ixworth to the storeroom. He was pacing in front of the lift, his eyes cast to the floor as he waited.

"Are you okay?" Chloe asked.

Ixworth looked up. "Oh, Chloe. Yes. I'm fine."

"You're sure?" said Chloe, watching him fold and unfold the paper three more times.

"Of course," he said as he stopped his pacing. He looked at her briefly and then his face softened. "Just one of those days when I have a lot on my mind. Have you ever had one of those? When you feel like you're drifting away from yourself or you can't get one thing straight before your head's racing off to think of something else?"

Chloe nodded. "I think so."

The lift arrived with a *ker-chunk*. Ixworth pulled the doors open, then turned to wave Chloe away.

"Go finish your chat with Maddox," he called. "There's no need to worry about me."

Chloe returned to the front of the shop. The foursome of tourists had left after purchasing a pack of tarot cards and dreamcatcher. Maddox had returned to the counter and was reading. The shop was quiet.

In the afternoon, dark clouds bullied away the sun and hovered lazily over the city, dispensing rain in small sporadic showers. Only a handful of shoppers ventured beyond their doorsteps.

"Is this violet or purple?" asked the shop's seventh and last customer of the day, holding out a patterned throw pillow. The elderly woman had entered the shop a quarter of an hour prior, dressed in a raincoat and wellies, just as Chloe was turning the final pages of *Braxton Bridle and the Cape Merrow Troll*. The woman announced herself as *it's-me-Eunice*. Chloe had seen her a number of times, as she was fond of the knickknacks the shop sold. Sometimes she would talk with Maddox, who was always happy and willing to discuss the particulars of anything.

"Purple, I think," answered Chloe, seeing as Maddox was busy behind the counter, feather-dusting a series of old photographs, and Ixworth, who had been secretive and quiet all afternoon, was still reading the paper he had been holding since coming in. Chloe wasn't sure there was a difference between the two colours.

"Right-then, I shall have it," Eunice said matter-of-factly. "Thank you, sugarplum." She paid Maddox with a wink and left without fanfare.

Chloe moved to the front window display. She pulled back a corner of the curtain and looked out. The rain had let up some, so she decided to head home. She bid farewell to Ixworth and Maddox and set out. Despite telling herself she had given up on the *Rosebud*, she found herself practising the motions on her way home. Maddox had said a lot of things that had left her feeling muddled. But now that she had some time to think about it, maybe it wasn't so confusing. Maddox had said making magic was similar to working on something creative like crafting a drawing or writing a story. What mattered was how she decided to do it for herself. Everybody was different. Chloe liked drawing. Maybe she just needed to like making magic. She promised herself she would practise in the coming days.

✦ ✦ ✦

When Chloe returned home from school on Monday, she found a small flyer sitting on the doormat. Picking it up, she read:

The Extraordinary Curiosities
of Ixworth and Maddox
London's finest collection of oddities,
peculiarities, mementoes, knick-knacks,
trinkets, gimmicks and what not.
We're far from common.
17 South Molton Lane, London, United Kingdom

The back of the flyer was blank. Chloe thought it odd Ixworth and Maddox would be sending out flyers but wouldn't mention it to her. It just seemed so modern. Turning the paper back over she noticed the words on the front had changed:

Excuse the theatrics of this silly flyer, Miss Chloe. Rest assured, only you will be able to read this note as it was intended. I was wondering if you could telephone me at your earliest convenience? It's a matter of great importance. I would have called on your mobile, but I didn't have the number. Very best,

— Maddox.

There was a number listed at the bottom of the flyer.

Chloe unlocked her front door and dropped her rucksack on the landing. She dialled. A telephone line buzzed hollowly as if the connection had been detoured through some distant offshore cable. Did Maddox own a telephone? Chloe couldn't recall having ever seen one in the shop.

Maddox answered after three rings: "This is Maddox."

"Maddox. It's Chloe. You left a note."

"Chloe!" said Maddox. "Thank goodness I've reached you. Is this a bad time?"

"It's fine," said Chloe. "I just got home from school."

"I know it seems a bit odd for me to be leaving strange notes on your door," replied the weird, tinny voice of Maddox. "But I was desperate to reach you. Rest assured the note was bewitched to go off and find you, wherever that may be. I have no knowledge of its discoveries."

"I don't mind if you know where I live," said Chloe. "What's wrong?"

"It's about Ixworth," said Maddox. "He's disappeared."

"Wait, what?" said Chloe. "What do you mean?"

"Just what I say," said Maddox. "He's disappeared. I'm worried sick."

"How do you know?" said Chloe.

"He didn't come in for work this morning," said Maddox.

"Are you sure he just didn't forget?" said Chloe. "He was acting a little strange yesterday."

"No-no," said Maddox. "He and I had talked about who would be covering today. I had some errands to run. He said he would mind the shop."

Maddox's connection chattered and clicked like a stray insect had gotten itself stuck somewhere in the line, and for a moment Chloe wondered if he had hung up.

"Maddox? Are you still there?"

"Sorry. I'm here," sighed Maddox. "Chloe—there's more. I found something else. I'm quite rattled."

Chloe was already moving toward the door. "You can tell me when I get there," she said hurriedly. "I'm on my way!"

✦ ✦ ✦

Chloe had once timed the journey from home to the curiosity shop. Nine minutes and fifty-seven seconds from door to door. Yet that afternoon, half walking, half running, Chloe could've sworn it felt like an hour. Maddox had sounded upset, and if Maddox was upset, then Chloe needed to be worried. Where was Ixworth?

"Have you heard from him?" gasped Chloe, bursting into the empty shop.

Maddox was standing near the register, his arms splayed out on the counter with his head down. He shook his head without looking up. "No. Nothing."

"Did you try calling him?" said Chloe.

"Several times," said Maddox. "There was no answer."

"Did you go by his house?" said Chloe. "Maybe he's fallen. Or been in an accident!"

"I was going to close the shop and run over there," said Maddox, his face going quite pale, "but then I found something else. And that stopped me."

Chloe's gut began to churn as if she had just swallowed something alive and whole and it had suddenly decided to start slithering around inside her stomach. "What? What did you find?"

"It's better if I just show you," said Maddox, taking a sheet of paper and a pen from one of the drawers. Hurriedly he scribbled, *Stepped-out for a quick bite. Back soon*, and taped the paper to the inside of the front window. He locked the shop door, turning back to face Chloe. "Come with me."

Chloe followed Maddox to the basement lift in the storeroom. He pulled back the metal grate, stepped inside and motioned for Chloe to follow. She hesitated. She had never been near the shop basement, aware it was home to the busyness of brownies.

"It's okay," said Maddox, noting Chloe's expression. "These are my premises, and you and I are friends. Nothing is off limits."

Chloe stepped into the lift, and Maddox closed the grate. To the right of the door was a rusted panel with two gold buttons, one on top of the other. Maddox pressed the bottom button, and the lift lurched to life, whirring and rumbling as the old metal groaned from its labours. For a moment there was only darkness beyond the lift grate, then the exposed skin of old brick, uneven and cracked. A pale light rose from below.

The lift stopped as suddenly as it had started. Maddox announced their arrival. He opened the grate, revealing a wide corridor. To the left, the walls were blackened like the brick had been scorched.

Maddox stepped away from the lift. Chloe followed. Along their right side, pegs lined the wall. Pegs to hang jackets. Brownie jackets. But only one jacket remained, one in navy blue tweed. It must have been Ixworth's. Maddox rounded a sharp corner into a small hallway. Ahead and to the right, tucked away in a small nook in the wall, was an old gramophone perched on a desk. An iron hat rack sat beside it.

"Four days ago, this was a bustling workshop," said Maddox. "Worktables, benches, beds. The brownie dormitory. "Now ..." His voice faltered. "Gone."

Chloe stared. A cavernous space lay just beyond the hall. It was near empty. "I don't understand. What happened to the brownies?"

Maddox held his elbow with his hand. "I was wondering that as well."

"Wait. You don't know?" said Chloe.

"No," said Maddox. "When I was last down here, there were nearly two dozen brownies working."

"When did they leave?" said Chloe.

"I don't know," said Maddox. "When Ixworth didn't come into the shop, I came down here looking for him. I thought he might have snuck in early to do some work."

Maddox waved one hand toward the empty space. "This is all that I found."

"This is crazy," said Chloe. "Weren't you here the whole time?"

"I was home," said Maddox, "in my flat. We had two showings last night: a Mr. Holmes of Kentish Town and Miss Constantine of Hamstead. Both were scheduled later than usual, but Ixworth volunteered to take care of them."

"And everything was gone this morning?" said Chloe.

"Indeed," said Maddox, shaking his head. "What I find most perplexing is this: how was it all taken away? It took us two months to set up this space. How did an entire workshop disappear overnight?"

"Magic?" offered Chloe.

Maddox frowned. "It would take a very powerful magician to do all this," he said, waving his hand.

"Was it Ixworth?" said Chloe. "Why would he just leave?"

"I can't think of a reason why he would just pack up all of his busyness without telling me," said Maddox. "Besides, Ixworth's *Flexure* is excellent. He knows me and could probably pop himself in and out of my realm without me knowing about it. But for him to move the entire workshop, brownies, furniture, supplies, tools—that's beyond his abilities."

Chloe walked the perimeter of the empty space. Little remained of the workshop Maddox had described save a few odds and ends: a pile of old bricks in one corner, a broken chair, dust and wood chips.

"It's funny," said Maddox sadly. "I just collected one of our *Toad Stools* for one of this week's displays. The brownies were still here!"

"Did you and Ixworth have a fight about something?" asked Chloe.

"Of course not," said Maddox, shaking his head. "We've always gotten along famously."

"Was he in danger? Maybe he had to leave because somebody's after him?" said Chloe.

"He's not in any trouble I know about," said Maddox. "Ixworth is a private person, but if he were in danger, he would have told me. Asked for my help."

Maddox led them back toward the lift. He stopped in front of Ixworth's jacket, which hung limply from its peg on the wall. "I suppose I should bring this back up to the shop," he said, removing it gingerly. Folding it under his arm, he walked to the lift and held the grate open for Chloe.

Chloe felt positively deflated. "What are we going to do?" she said, stepping inside.

"I'll go around his house after I've closed the shop," Maddox said solemnly. "I have an early showing that I probably shouldn't cancel. Maybe this is all just a big mix-up." He pulled the grate closed and pushed the up button on the panel inside the door. The lift jolted to life.

As the lift shuddered and groaned upward, Chloe was suddenly aware of a musty odour rising up from the shaft beneath them. Sour and hot, it left her with an impression that all was not right.

CHAPTER 8

MR. THIRSK

Chloe's heart sank as she turned onto Wood's Mews. A bright silver sedan was parked in front of the house. Chloe recognized it immediately: Aunt Jean and Uncle Jon were visiting.

Chloe took a deep breath as she came through the front door. There were loud voices and laughter coming from the kitchen. Judging by the ruckus of pots and pans, Mum was making a fuss. She always did when company came over. Chloe slumped in to join them.

Between hugs from Aunt Jean and light jabs on the shoulder from Uncle Jon, Chloe learned that they had just arrived in London, a spontaneous visit prompted by all three of their children going away to school at the same time. This lack of cousins offered Chloe some relief. The youngest cousin, Neil, had a habit of pinching for no reason. Mum and her sister Jean had already shifted to their big voices: louder and more blustery versions of their regular ones. Chloe wondered if Mum was aware of the switch; it had a strange affect on Dad. As she grew louder, he got quieter, which may have been the reason she did it.

Mum and Jean talked endlessly through the dinner. Chloe fidgeted, desperate for news from Maddox. Had he gone to Ixworth's house yet? Why hadn't he called? Chloe kept checking her mobile, taking it out of her pocket, looking, then putting it back. Mum finally leaned over and took it away. "You can have it back after dinner," she said crossly. "Honestly, Chlo'. How often do we have company?"

Chloe stewed in silence as Dad and Jon talked about their football matches and Mum and Jean relived a summer trip to the Isle of White. It was the longest meal Chloe could remember. Afterward, they all gathered in the living room to talk even more. When the cards and coffee were brought out, Chloe was allowed to excuse herself. She slunk tiredly to her room.

It was half eight. The sun was setting, bathing Chloe's room in cosy evening light. After checking her mobile for messages, she sank beside the window, peering out. The neighbour's cat crept stealthily beneath the hydrangeas in the front garden. Something had frightened her away from her usual perch near the iron gate at the front of the house. A man. Chloe had seen him before. The one with the long slick hair who had followed her from the shop.

Quickly she drew the curtain.

Chloe was shaking. How had he found her? Taking a breath, she braved another look: the man remained, his back to the gate.

Should she tell Mum and Dad?

Just then, the man looked up toward her window.

He was thin and wiry, like a skeleton, with white hair pulled back in a tight ponytail. His dirty coat looked like it had been pulled up from the bottom of the Thames. But it was his smile that made Chloe shiver. His teeth seemed longer than they should have been, and there were too many, like a shark's mouth. The man held up a bony finger, waving it back and forth. No. Then he vanished. Pop. A light going out in a dark room.

She was being followed by a magician.

Chloe dialled Maddox on her mobile with shaking hands. This was too much. She was frightened and needed to speak to him now. The line rang hollowly, but Maddox didn't pick up. She tried three more times, yet each time was the same.

Chloe paced the length of her room. Had Maddox gone missing too? She needed to go check. But leaving now would be a problem. Mum would never let her out this late. Plus, the creepy man was following her. Chloe shivered again. She was crazy for even thinking of leaving. But if the man was a magician, then the house wasn't safe. Only Maddox could help. She could go by the shop quick, slip out while the grownups were distracted. If she were caught, she could just say she went out for a bit of air. Or maybe she could go after Mum and Dad went to bed? Maybe she could dress one of her pillows in clothes so it looked like she was still sleeping in her bed. No. That wouldn't work. It would never fool Mum. This was her only chance. She needed to go right now.

Chloe packed Ixworth's jar of *Crummock Water* in

her rucksack. It had saved her once; it might just do it again. She left her room and closed the door quietly behind her. Uncle Jon was in the middle of telling a story about how he had locked his keys in the car with the engine running. The grownups were distracted. Chloe slipped past the living room unseen and crept down the stairs to the foyer. She was out the door before she could talk herself out of this madness.

There was no sign of the strange man as Chloe sneaked down the front walk. She moved slowly to the gate, scanning the street left and right. When she was sure it was clear, she tightened her rucksack straps and set off at a jog. The sun had set brilliantly, delaying nightfall's approach with rays of golden light. Chloe passed only a few people. Nobody paid her any notice.

When Chloe arrived at the shop, it was dark. Oddly, the sign in the window had been replaced with a new one: *Closed for inventory.*

Chloe knocked on the shop door.

She waited. Five minutes passed.

She pulled her mobile from the pocket of her hoodie and dialled. The line rang a dozen times or more. She was about to hang up when someone answered.

"Yes?" croaked a voice.

"Maddox?"

"Chloe!" coughed Maddox.

"Why didn't you call me?" Chloe said crossly. "Did you find Ixworth?"

"I'm sorry," said Maddox before exploding into another fit of coughing.

"You sound sick," said Chloe.

"To be honest, I don't feel quite myself right now."

"The front door's locked," said Chloe. "I can't get in."

"The front door?" said Maddox. There was a long pause. "Oh! You're here. Why are you out so late?"

"I came to find out about Ixworth," said Chloe. "And something else. I think another magician is following me."

The line hissed and crackled. "Wait just a moment," said Maddox. "I'll come get you."

It was several minutes before Maddox appeared inside the shop door. After some difficulty with the latch, he ushered Chloe in, ensuring the door was locked behind him. He had a tired, weary look about his eyes, and he was dressed in a maroon housecoat and slippers. Chloe stared at him with concern.

"Forgive my appearance," he said. "I'm a little under-the-weather."

"You are sick," said Chloe.

"No," said Maddox, "just tired. I overexerted myself."

"What does that mean?" said Chloe, trying to sound sweet but feeling cross.

Maddox moved behind the register, leaning heavily on the counter. "You said a magician followed you to your house?"

"Yes," said Chloe, "I think it's the same one who followed me the other night after work. He showed up in front of the house tonight. And then he vanished. Right in front of me!"

"You've seen him before?" Maddox tutted. "Why didn't you say something?"

"I felt silly," Chloe said sheepishly. "I didn't want you to think I needed babysitting."

"Miss Chloe," Maddox said sternly, "you're not silly, and I don't think you need babysitting. If something like this happens again, promise me you'll tell me about it. Promise?"

Chloe nodded.

"Now, how did he disappear?" said Maddox. "A slow fading away, or more of one quick blink and gone?"

"Definitely a blink and gone," said Chloe. "One moment he was standing at the gate, the next—nothing."

Maddox stroked his beard. His hair was in disarray, as if he'd spent the entire night on some bleary windswept coast. "Did you happen to see what he looked like?"

"Old," said Chloe with a nod. "Greasy hair. Weird teeth. A long jacket. Kind of like a hobo."

Maddox sighed tiredly.

"What's wrong with you?" said Chloe. "You're acting weird. Why won't you tell me what happened at Ixworth's?"

"I just did a bit too much," said Maddox.

"That's a lie," said Chloe. "What really happened?"

Maddox took a moment to collect his thoughts. "I went to Ixworth's."

"You already told me you were going," said Chloe, taking a step closer to the counter. "Did he say why he left without telling you?"

Maddox winced as if reliving a painful memory. "I never made it to his house."

"What do you mean?" said Chloe.

Maddox massaged his temples with the tips of his fingers. "I got as far as Knightsbridge and then I was *Evicted.*"

Chloe waited for further explanation, but when Maddox didn't elaborate, she prodded, "That's bad, right?"

"Generally speaking," said Maddox. "Essentially, a magician is the landlord of his realm. He can *Evict* anyone he chooses, even other magicians."

"Why would Ixworth *Evict* you?" said Chloe. "You're friends."

"I don't know," said Maddox. "I'm not even sure it was him. It was a very strong spell."

"How do you know?" said Chloe.

Maddox chuckled softly before exploding into a fit of coughing. "Look at me, Miss Chloe. I'm a right mess. I was *Evicted* so suddenly I'm still trying to come to terms with it. It was a very precise, very strong *Eviction*. I never thought Ixworth had it in him."

Chloe looked at Maddox again, stooped over the counter in his housecoat. "Do you have someone to look after you?" she said finally.

Maddox smiled politely. "Mr. Winch has been taking good care of me since my return. This house coat was his idea. Bless him. I'll have to write to his family and tell them what a fine job he's doing."

Maddox stood up slowly.

"Now about that other matter. Just hold on, I'll be right back." He shuffled slowly to the rear of the shop. He was gone for nearly a quarter of an hour, and by then

Chloe had started to wonder if he had succumbed to the effects of the *Eviction*. When he returned, he was holding a brown paper package. He handed it to Chloe.

"What is it?" said Chloe, holding it tightly.

"A little something for the fellow who's bothering you," said Maddox. "If he is a magician like you say, it will do the trick. At least for a day or two."

Chloe examined the package closely. There was nothing threatening about it. "What do I do with it?"

"You don't have to do anything, m'dear," said Maddox. "If this mysterious magician makes another appearance at your house, just tear away the brown paper."

"And then what?" said Chloe.

"Nothing," said Maddox. "The package will take care of the rest."

✦ ✦ ✦

It was a quarter to ten by the time Chloe left the curiosity shop. The streets were dark. Only grownups were about, off to late meals, midnight shows, and all the other places grown-ups flock to after children are in bed. Chloe was less worried about the weird magician than she was about being out after dark. Mum would be mad. Actually, not mad, that was too mild a word. *Furious*. Chloe would never be allowed out of the house again if she were caught. Luckily, there had been no frantic calls to Chloe's mobile, so she knew she hadn't been found out yet. But getting back inside the house was going to be tricky. As Chloe approached the house, she wasn't sure if she was glad Aunt Jean and Uncle Jon's car was still parked at the curb. It meant Mum and Dad were still distracted. But what if their guests were leaving? Mum had a habit of long drawn-out goodbyes. If they were all huddled in the foyer, Chloe was finished.

Chloe slipped through the gate and approached the house cautiously. She bent, putting her ear to the door. All seemed quiet on the other side. Holding her breath, she turned the handle, pushing the door open slowly. *Squeak,* sang a duet of hinges in tiny mouse voices. Chloe froze, listening for the sound of hurried footsteps on the stairs. Nothing. When she was sure no one was coming, she pushed the door all the way open and stepped inside.

Mum and Aunt Jean were laughing from somewhere upstairs. Chloe allowed herself to breathe. Removing her rucksack, she took to the stairs quietly.

"Chlo," called Dad, "is that you?"

Chloe froze. Looking up, she could see the silhouette of Dad standing at the top of the stairs. "I thought you were in bed?"

Chloe marched up the stairs trying to act natural. "I was," she said. "And then I remembered something. A project. I forgot." She held out Maddox's package. "I left this in my school bag. See?"

Dad was holding a bowl of crisps. He had been walking and eating, judging by the crumbs on his shirt collar. He noted Chloe's package and nodded sagely. "Not another permission form, then?" he said.

"Nope," said Chloe, squeezing by. She paused on the threshold of the kitchen. "Having fun, Dad?"

Dad bit into another crisp and nodded.

"Good," said Chloe. "I'm off to bed. "G'night."

Chloe tidied her bookshelf and found a place for Maddox's package. The contents, whimsical, otherworldly, toxic, she couldn't begin to guess. Yet clearly it was a thing of magic, for when she held it, she had a sense that tucked away inside was something extraordinary. It was a strange thing to put her faith in something so ordinary, yet the package became a symbol of hope. For Chloe knew it was there to protect her from the mysterious magician who was wandering the streets of Mayfair looking for her.

✦ ✦ ✦

"Feeling better?" said Chloe, when she came into the shop on Tuesday.

"Nearly," said Maddox. "I'm still a bit woolly in the head, but I think by tomorrow I'll have made a full recovery."

"Have you heard anything from Ixworth?" asked Chloe. She had been worrying about him all day and had come to the shop directly from school. She had wanted to ask that first, but it seemed rude not to ask Maddox how he was doing.

"No, nothing," said Maddox, shaking his head sadly. "I've been thinking about it, trying to piece it together. I'm at wit's end. The unknowing is the worst thing."

Chloe tried to think of something comforting to say while fumbling with the strap on her rucksack.

"Still have that package I gave you?" said Maddox, trying to change the subject.

"On my bookshelf. Safe," said Chloe.

"And this magician you suspect is following you. Any sign of him?"

"Not so far."

"Good," said Maddox. "Listen, I think I have an idea who it is, judging by your description, that is. It sounds as if it could be Mr. Thirsk."

"Who is he?" said Chloe, shuddering at the memory of the strange, greasy man.

"A magician, like you guessed," said Maddox. "His realm is south of the river: Vauxhall to Battersea. A few streets toward South Bank. I've only met him once or twice in passing, but there are stories."

"I had a feeling you were going to say that," said Chloe miserably.

"Now hold on," said Maddox. "There's no need to panic. You're safe. This is my realm, and I won't let anything happen to you. Besides, we still don't *know* he's following you. Perhaps this is just a strange coincidence."

"You said there were stories about Mr. Thirsk," said Chloe. "What's he done?"

Maddox looked at Chloe mildly, trying not to alarm her. "Questionable things."

"You can tell me. I'm not afraid," said Chloe resolutely.

"I wasn't suggesting you were, Miss Chloe," said

Maddox. "I just don't want you to worry about yet another thing. To be honest, there isn't much to tell. Just rumours, mostly. He has a reputation for not getting along with other magicians. There have been a few disagreements over the years that have ended under suspicious circumstances."

"What does that mean?" said Chloe.

Maddox smiled kindly. "If you must know, let's just say it's not a coincidence Mr. Thirsk has one of the largest realms in the city."

"So he takes other people's realms?" asked Chloe.

Maddox looked uncomfortable. "Stealing another magician's realm is forbidden. There are rules. That's why the Redistributing and Appropriation Act of the Magicians' Chartulary was put in place. To stop us from fighting over territory."

"I don't have a realm," said Chloe. "What would Mr. Thirsk want with me?"

"That's what we need to find out," said Maddox. "But first we need to establish that it really is him. This fellow is using some sneaky magic to allow him to come into Mayfair without me realising."

"Can you *Evict* him?" said Chloe.

"I can—that is, if I can pick up on his activities. He's devious. Usually a magician can sense when another is snooping about his realm. I'm not sure how he's going about it. Perhaps a variation of an *Obliquitous Chasse* ..."

"I have no idea what that means," said Chloe. "Do you think this has something to do with me knowing about your shop?"

"Why would that have anything to do with it?" asked Maddox.

"Maybe regular people aren't allowed to work with magicians?" said Chloe.

"Of course they are," said Maddox. "Why would anybody be bothered by that? Rest assured, there is no such rule. To tell you the truth, I don't know why another magician would be interested in you. Just be prepared to use that package should he come back to your house. Speaking of which, I've made something smaller for you to carry around. Something you can tuck away in a pocket. Just to be safe."

Maddox presented Chloe with a small velvet jewellery box. His instructions were clear: "Keep this with you at all times until further notice. If you're approached by Thirsk, don't talk to him. Open the lid to the box and get away as fast as you can. This is only a temporary measure."

Chloe took some comfort in this and did as Maddox instructed. The velvet jewellery box became part of her dressing routine. Sweater. Skirt. Plimsolls. Rucksack. Oyster Card. Jewellery box. She carried it with her at home, when about, and at school.

On Thursday, Chloe wrote her final exam of the school year. She hadn't studied as much as normal. But things had been busy and weird. At least she'd managed to answer all the questions. When finished, she put her pen down on her desk with finality. Finished. Around her, many of her classmates were still writing, frantically scratching at their papers in the final minutes. Normally, she would be concerned about her grades, but she had other things on her mind. Mr. Thirsk and Ixworth—especially Ixworth. It was tiring worrying about someone all the time.

Chloe spent much of the first official day of summer wondering how she could help Maddox. The strange *Eviction* kept him away from Ixworth's realm. How were they going to find out if Ixworth was okay? Surely magic was the answer. And Chloe had none. She needed to perfect her *Rosebud*. Enough was enough.

After lunch, Chloe made her way to the garden. It seemed safe territory to practise magic, as it was away from the road and only accessible from the house. And hopefully out of sight from spying magicians. Chloe paced between the butterfly bushes, trying to remember the moves of the *Rosebud*. Pinch thumb and index finger. Clockwise left. Counter clockwise right. Pull fingers apart—hot toffee. She practised these actions several times until she could do them effortlessly without thinking. Maddox had added to his instructions: "One needs to place something inside a *Rosebud* to make it work properly." Chloe surveyed the yard looking for something to add to her spell. It was a tidy space, free of litter and leaves, every branch and stem trimmed and in place. The pear tree Mum complained about endlessly was nearby. Chloe approached, grasping one of the leaves between her outstretched fingers. She wondered what to do next. What had Maddox meant by adding to the spell?

Something suddenly *popped*.

An instant later, a puff of green smoke began to form in the palm of Chloe's hand. She stared at the wafting form, amazed. It was no larger than the head of a mushroom, but real, alive, with a clear sense of purpose about it. She knew without a doubt she was holding a *Rosebud*.

The smoke cleared, revealing a kernel of light: otherworldly blue, too bright to be bright, and too dim to be dim. The thing bobbled playfully in Chloe's hand. She poked it gently with the tip of her finger, and the light quivered excitedly.

Heart pounding, Chloe knelt, guiding the light to the base of the pear tree. Gently, she set it down in the soil around the trunk. A thought suddenly formed in her head: *Grow*.

Chloe should have been excited. It was her first *Rosebud*! Conjured on her own, without any help. But what happened next was not what she expected.

✦ ✦ ✦

"I'm mad at you," said Chloe, glaring at Maddox three quarters of an hour later.

"Oh?" said Maddox, who was flipping through an old book near the register. "I'm sure it won't be the last time."

"That spell you gave me didn't work," said Chloe.

"The jewellery box won't work if you don't keep it with you," said Maddox anxiously.

"Not that, the *Rosebud*!"

"Oh, that's not a spell. I just gave you instructions."

"You said a spell is just a *Rosebud* with something inside."

Maddox stopped reading. "Oh dear, what did you do?"

"I killed Mum's pear tree."

"Just a tree?" asked Maddox.

"Mum loved that tree," sighed Chloe.

"Well, I'm sure she did, but let's be thankful; it could have been so much worse."

"I turned the tree to ash. The whole thing. Like a burnt piece of toast. How could it be worse?" said Chloe.

"You could have put out an eye," said Maddox.

"That's not funny," said Chloe.

"I'm serious," said Maddox. "One wrong move, a cough, a slightly mispronounced word. Replace something with such-and-such, pill for ill, tomato-potato and you could end up hurting someone."

Chloe stared at her feet.

"What did you put in the *Rosebud?*" said Maddox.

"How am I supposed to know?" said Chloe.

"When you cast the spell, what were you thinking about?"

"I was thinking I wanted the pear tree to grow."

"And were you specific?" said Maddox.

"That is specific," Chloe said irritably.

Maddox sighed. "I really have failed you," he said. "One must be thorough when casting spells. You need to be very precise. You go around telling plants to grow, and that's what they'll do. In your case, your Mother's pear tree grew all at once. Each little cell giving it their all. *Everything*. No wonder it turned to ash. The whole thing burned itself out."

Chloe thought of spells for the remainder of the afternoon. She should have known better. Ixworth had told her to be specific when using the *Crummock Water*. She should have remembered. Magic was such a finicky thing. It wasn't like a problem with arithmetic where one could return to the problem and discover the mistake. Everything had to be in the moment. And while Maddox thought his lectures were helpful, they were only making her frustrated.

By some miracle, the burnt pear tree had yet to be discovered when Chloe returned home. She wondered what she should tell Mum: maybe explain that she had spilled something on it? *Acid? Fire?* Luckily, Dad surprised Mum with a dinner reservation at her favourite restaurant in an attempt to make up for a forgotten anniversary, which gave Chloe another day to think of an excuse.

Chloe was alone again for the evening. She had a frozen dinner in front of the television. She put on a movie, but didn't watch it. She was feeling helpless and sad. Even going to the shop to see Maddox that afternoon hadn't helped. When she was there, they didn't talk about Ixworth, but Chloe knew he was on both of their minds.

At half seven, there was a knock at the door. It wasn't loud, yet the sound of it, the sharpness and authority of the rapping, echoed through the house like a gong strike. Chloe froze.

Thirsk had finally announced himself.

Chloe got up, knocking over the remains of her dinner. She raced for the stairs.

When the second knock arrived, it nearly dropped her to the floor. Then there came a sound. Not a voice nor a spoken word. A *thrum*. Like a deep rumbling drum that rolled up to attack Chloe's senses, a pressing down on her chest and shouting its clear meaning: "*Open-up-open-up-open-up-open-up ....*"

CHAPTER 9

AMOROUS

Chloe stumbled into her room as the knocking came again. She suddenly felt a terrible urge to obey the summons, as if something sinister had been cast by the rapping knuckles. *Answer the door.* Chloe reached her bookshelf. Taking Maddox's package in hand, she clawed desperately at the paper.

Knock. Knock. Knock.

Chloe's body quivered. Without knowing why, she started moving toward her bedroom door. *Whoever was calling needed to be let in.*

The package in her hand was a sudden reminder she was in danger. Thirsk must have been using magic to summon her. She knew the next knock would be worse. She focused again on the package—the paper was nearly off.

Thirsk hammered on the door again. *Open-open-open-open* the knocking demanded. Chloe felt a tug pulling at her muscles and compelling her to walk down the stairs.

Then everything was quiet again. Forcing herself to the window, she peered between the curtains. Mr. Thirsk had withdrawn to the gate, his long jacket blending into the pavement like a shadow. He looked up, meeting her eyes. With a wicked smile, he made a move back toward the door. With little time to lose, Chloe tore the last of the wrapping from Maddox's package. A plain cardboard box with a lid lay beneath. Clenching teeth, she opened it.

Something miraculous emerged from the package: a force like a whirling storm. It lingered for only a moment, fluttering about and then—*whoosh*—it tore from the room, leaving a strange sadness in its wake, like a very special someone had just left the party one was attending. As the spell blustered through the house, it began to break apart, seeping through cracks and squeezing under doorways and windows, trying desperately to escape.

Outside, the willowy wisps of the spell came back together, churning violently above Mr. Thirsk in a galaxy-like flurry. As it frothed and boiled, it grew stronger. A moment later, the cloud descended upon him, grasping and clawing at his frock coat.

And then quite suddenly, everything stopped. Mr. Thirsk was left standing in his boot-steps, flustered, but unharmed.

Chloe could feel the panic rising. "It didn't work," she moaned to herself. She stared down at the open package in her arms. She didn't have anything else to defend herself. "The jewellery box!" she said, suddenly remembering the added protection Maddox had prepared for her. She paused at the window. Something was happening below.

On the street below, Mr. Thirsk was in the middle of a cat-wash of straightening his jacket and smoothing his frazzled hair. Around him, there was movement: a discarded paper cup, the tattered pages of a newspaper, an old worn-out mitten. All began to move toward the unsuspecting man.

Mr. Thirsk only became aware of the situation when the remains of a half-eaten sandwich shuffled lovingly onto the toe of his boot. With a look of panic, he backed away from the house as the objects advanced, and then turning quickly, he walked hurriedly eastward along the street.

The rubbish heap continued to grow. An old tire joined the ranks. A broken rake, a pile of grass cuttings, apple cores, cabbage leaves, frozen dinner trays, cans, bottles, crisp packages, the back of an antique chair, several off-colour piles of a questionable substance, and other waste from Wood's Mews and many of the surrounding streets. The rubbish rushed forward, a wave of debris clinging to Mr. Thirsk's pant legs, swarming about him, grasping like clawing hands.

Mr. Thirsk cast several defensive spells, which tossed aside the rubbish temporarily, giving him a few breaths to run farther. The effect only lasted a moment, and the attack resumed. Push away. Come back. Push away. Come back.

When Mr. Thirsk reached the corner of Wood's Mews, he was unrecognisable for the waste stuck to his skinny frame. And then he was gone, turning the corner in a mad rush to return to his realm.

Despite the seriousness of the situation, Chloe couldn't help smiling. Maddox had really come through. Mr. Thirsk seemed quite ridiculous at that moment. She was tempted to run over to the shop and thank Maddox, but just then Mum and Dad returned home from dinner. It would have to wait until tomorrow.

✦ ✦ ✦

"What was the name of that spell?" asked Chloe when she arrived at the shop the next day.

Maddox was at the counter. He was holding the same book he had been reading all week. Chloe noted the title written along the spine. *Deconstructing Evictions* by Almeric Krell.

"Which spell?" he said mildly without looking up.

"You know. The one in the package."

Maddox slammed his book shut abruptly. "I thought I heard the calling of my sweet Mayfair," he said with a sly grin. "My magic was on the move, yes?"

Chloe couldn't help but giggle at his enthusiasm. "I unwrapped the package, if that's what you mean," she said. "It worked perfectly. What was inside?"

Maddox clucked. "That was a variation of an *Amorous*."

"A love potion?" asked Chloe, thinking *Amorous* sounded a lot like a French word she had heard in school once.

"A like potion," corrected Maddox.

"What's the difference?" said Chloe.

Maddox drummed his fingers on the countertop. "There is no doubt Mr. Thirsk is a powerful magician," he began, "But this is my realm. I am the master, and I make the rules. So, using the familiarity I have with my home, I created a spell that, once released, made portions of my realm attracted to him."

Chloe stared blankly at Maddox, expecting him to say something else. "I don't think I understand," she said finally. "Parts of your realm? Which parts?"

"Mostly the rubbish," said Maddox with a toothy smile.

Chloe giggled again. "I never opened the jewellery box. What's inside that?"

"A similar spell but with a twist," said Maddox. "It's paired with the one inside the package. It will be more potent now that the first spell has taken effect. That is, if Thirsk decides to bother you again. But I don't think he will."

"So he's gone forever?" said Chloe.

"Sadly not," said Maddox, shaking his head. "It will take Thirsk some time to work his way out of that first bit of magic. He'll be fine when he's back in his realm, but if he tries anything here, he'll be feeling it again. That is until he figures out how to untangle the magic. Any good magician can deconstruct a spell. It just takes time."

"I know I ask too many questions," said Chloe, "but what happens if he comes back and I need to use the jewellery box? How will it work if Mr. Thirsk has untangled the spell from the package?"

Maddox clapped his hands together silently. "Like I said, there's a twist. Given enough time, one can prepare for anything. In this case, I've added something unexpected, something out of the ordinary, keeping in mind I know Thirsk will attempt to deconstruct the original spell, probably by methods similar to the way I would. So I set a trap, of sorts. Just a slight adjustment."

Chloe was enjoying thinking of something blowing up in Thirsk's face. "What's the trap?"

"He'll try to untangle himself," said Maddox with a smirk. "In other words, try to stop the spell from being attracted to him. But I added something I like to call *A Scorned Sweetheart*. You might have seen something similar in films or read about it in story books. Basically it's what happens when someone wants to stop being another person's sweetheart and the other person doesn't take kindly to it. And they end up—*ahem*—acting unreasonably. Savagely in some cases. In essence, the outcome will be much the same as the original spell."

"Making adjustments to spells sounds complicated," said Chloe. "I don't think I'll ever get to that level."

"Nonsense," cried Maddox. "It's just a matter of tweaking the order of the recipe. A simmering of entanglements, so to speak."

"I have no idea what you're talking about," said Chloe.

"Elementary spell casting, m'dear."

"It may be elementary," said Chloe sighing, "but I've only managed a *Rosebud* once."

"It's a good start," said Maddox.

Chloe thought for a moment. "I want you to teach me," she said resolutely.

"I thought I was teaching you," said Maddox.

"No. I mean really teach me," said Chloe.

"My instructions have been a far cry better than what I received from my master," said Maddox. "Now, he was a poor teacher. And a devil, perhaps. Oh yes, definitely that."

"I'm talking about lessons," said Chloe. "not practising. The next time I come in, you can tell me what I'm doing wrong. Maybe show me how to fix it. And once I know how to do a *Rosebud* properly, you can show me how to add things to it."

Maddox thought about this for a long moment. "It would be helpful to have another magician," he said. "What with all that's happened. You could prove useful."

"Yes, exactly," said Chloe.

"Self preservation as well," said Maddox.

"What do you mean?"

"Well," said Maddox with a smile. "After hearing what you did to your poor mother's pear tree, I'm worried you may do the same to me."

Chloe took to practising her *Rosebud* like a person possessed. It helped her with her feelings of helplessness and was a way of making her feel like she was making progress. If she became a capable magician, perhaps she wouldn't be so afraid of Mr. Thirsk. Maybe she could even help Maddox in his search for Ixworth. Alone in her room, she decided to create a *Rosebud* her own way. Isn't that what Maddox recommended? Each magician approaches magic in their own way? She envisioned making toast. All the little details about it: the thickness of the bread, the colour of the crust, the way the butter melted and dripped along one side. It was working. Chloe's fingers started to take to the motions, like they knew what to do before she did. Soon it was a smooth effortless motion, fanned fingers, tiny soldiers jumping into a pool, smallest to tallest.

When Chloe got up on Thursday, she had three voicemail messages from Maddox.

7:52: *"Hullo Miss Ashley. It's Maddox. Listen, I've discovered something. I think it's important. Would you mind giving me a ring when you can?"*

8:03: *"Hullo-hullo-hullo, Chloe. Just leaving you another message in case you didn't receive my last one. You did, right? It's Maddox. Ring me please?"*

8:23: *"Heavens! Aren't you up yet? Who sleeps this late? Ring me. It's about Ixworth!"*

Chloe didn't even bother calling Maddox back. As soon as Mum left for work, Chloe was off.

The shop was locked when Chloe arrived. The temporary *Closed for inventory* still hung crookedly in the window. Chloe knocked. Maddox answered straight away as if he had been waiting behind the door.

"What have you found?" said Chloe, coming into the shop behind Maddox.

"Remember when I showed you the empty workshop?" said Maddox, opening a drawer and removing something from within. "Ixworth's jacket was left on one of the pegs. Remember?"

"I remember," said Chloe.

"Right," said Maddox. "I found this in the pocket." Maddox held a piece of paper between his fingers. It was winkled along the edges from being folded and unfolded too many times. He placed it on the counter, smoothing it with his palm. Chloe recognized it as the one Ixworth had been rereading obsessively the day before he disappeared. Maddox pointed at the slip of paper.

"Judging by its colour and texture, it appears to be a copy of *the Quarterly Crow*," he said. "But I can't be sure."

"What do you mean, you can't be sure?" said Chloe.

Maddox glanced at the paper, wincing.

"What's wrong?" said Chloe.

"I don't know," said Maddox. "It hurts if I try to read it. Even look at it, actually."

"Hurts you?" said Chloe. "That's weird."

"Yes, I've tried and tried to unravel it, whatever it is, without any luck."

Chloe slowly reached a hand out. "Let me try."

Maddox was hesitant, but Chloe insisted. "I can do it," she said.

Maddox handed Chloe the bulletin, and she scanned the rough paper.

"I can read it fine," she said.

"Really?" said Maddox, "Which *Crow* is it? The date's below the banner at the top."

"Says Spring Edition," said Chloe.

"Right-right," said Maddox. "I have a copy of that myself. Three articles: the first is about the disappearance of Mr. Brockwell, if memory serves me correctly."

Chloe checked the headlines:

Mr. Brockwell Missing from Wandsworth After Nightly Trek Along Causeway.
Next Guild Meeting Scheduled for September 24th
Tickets to Snaith Station Lost: Feared Found by Non Magicians.

"Wait! There are four articles, not three," said Chloe. "The last article repeats itself. The same words over and over." She flipped the page, "onto the other side too."

Maddox stroked his beard. "Would you mind reading it to me?"

Chloe nodded. She read:

Case Miraculously Solved!

It was recently determined that two elderly magicians who had attended a dinner party at Oswin Blythe's residence died from eating a hearty, well-salted cabbage soup. The magicians both held titles to realms within central London."A terrible-terrible tragedy," Mr. Blythe was quoted as saying. "Cabbage is funny that way. One never knows when it's going to go off. It's a good thing it doesn't agree with me. Never has. Otherwise this story might have been about the death of three magicians."

"Dinner party?" said Maddox, "Magicians who died from eating cabbage soup? Titles in central London? No-no-no. That can't be right. No such thing ever happened! This must be some kind of joke."

"I still don't understand why you can't read it," said Chloe, handing the paper back to Maddox.

"It makes little sense to me as well," sighed Maddox. "When I try, it feels like ... I'm struggling to come up with the right way to say it. Like it's not mine to read. Like it wasn't meant for my eyes, if that makes any sense?"

Chloe nodded and the two were silent for a long while. Maddox folded the paper and stowed it back in the drawer behind the counter.

"Is it a clue?" Chloe said finally.

"I think it is," said Maddox. "I'll admit, there have been times when I feared Ixworth cast aside our friendship. After all, magicians are solitary creatures. Each of us is bound to our realm, and realms can't be shared. It tends to keep us apart."

"But you and Ixworth have been friends for so long," said Chloe. "Why would he give that up?"

"That's what I've been struggling with," said Maddox.

Chloe thought suddenly of her friend Iris. Lately, she'd been feeling that their friendship wasn't the same as it always had been. "Do you think Ixworth left deliberately?"

"Not any longer," said Maddox, placing his hand on the counter. "This discovery—this strange alternate version of *the Quarterly Crow*—Ixworth was obsessed with it. Do you remember he couldn't let it go the day he disappeared? I thought maybe he was just preoccupied with the running of the business. But no, this means something. Something about it isn't right. I think somebody had something to do with his disappearance."

CHAPTER 10

FISHING

Chloe was spending nearly all of her free time with Maddox. The discovery of the strange news bulletin had given her hope that maybe they would find Ixworth and things would go back to the way they had been.

"Why haven't you sent Mr. Winch to check up on Ixworth's house?" said Chloe as they headed south on Davis Street. They had nipped out for a spot of takeaway, as Maddox had been feeling cooped up and in need of something nice. A tidy curry seemed to fit the bill.

"I was worried he might get *Evicted*," said Maddox, holding their food close to his chest as if it were an infant in need of warmth. "I would hate for anything bad to happen to him. He's been such a good chap through all of this."

"Do you really think Ixworth is behind the *Eviction?*" said Chloe.

"I've wondered about that," said Maddox. "I find it hard to believe Ixworth would *Evict* me on purpose."

"Could it have been someone else?" said Chloe.

"No," said Maddox. "Unless, of course, someone

has taken over his realm and performed the *Eviction* themself, but that is unlikely."

"Would you be able to tell?" said Chloe recalling Maddox's run-down appearance after his *Eviction*.

"It takes time to assume another's realm," Maddox explained. "The relationship between a magician and his or her home is deeply personal. It takes time for the bond to become strong. Besides, each of us has a certain—what's the word?—Taste? Flavour?—to our magic. We put it together differently. Someone posing as Ixworth would have to be truly great considering how well I know him and his methods."

"Why don't I go?" said Chloe.

"Absolutely not," said Maddox.

"I want to," said Chloe. "Ixworth is my friend too. I want to help."

Maddox turned to Chloe; when he spoke, his tone was soft: "I'll admit, the thought did cross my mind," he said. "However, I can't be sure it's safe. Someone is trying to stop people from going to Ixworth's house. I can't risk you. Too many things could go wrong."

Chloe was silent for a moment, hurt that this decision had been made for her. "Do you have any idea how the whole workshop got moved in just a day?"

"None," said Maddox as they turned onto South Molten Lane. "I'm flummoxed."

"Is it possible ...?" said Chloe.

"Is what possible?" said Maddox.

Chloe swallowed, unsure how to say it. "Is it possible somebody snuck into the workshop without you or

Ixworth knowing? Maybe he was kidnapped?"

Maddox stopped. "I've considered this many times. We already know Thirsk has managed to come and go without me knowing, but to break into the shop using magic, like a *Flexure,* would be like someone ringing an alarm. It would be very hard to conceal."

"You would have sensed it, right?" said Chloe.

"Yes," said Maddox, mentally chewing the porridge of his words "Sensed. Or ... sniffed."

"Sniffed?"

Maddox perked up, staring off toward the antique market across from the shop as if he had suddenly gained the ability to see through the walls and was now comparing the items within to those in his tiny shop.

"What's the matter?" said Chloe, noting his odd expression.

"I'm thinking," Maddox said flatly.

"Yes, I noticed. About what?"

Maddox turned to look at her. "Miss Chloe: How would you like to go fishing?"

* * *

It was clear to Chloe she had overdressed. She had worn wellies and a warm jacket, clothing appropriate for her idea of fishing, although her knowledge of the subject was little. Fishing was standing outside, peering down into murky water, shooing away midges, and, perhaps, worms.

"What exactly are we doing?" said Chloe, filing

behind Maddox into the empty basement workshop. It was the first time she had been back since Ixworth and the brownies had disappeared.

"I've already told you what we're doing," said Maddox. He set a small brown suitcase on the floor beside him and tapped it with his foot. "Why are you dressed like that again?"

Chloe gave him a dismissive eye roll. "Is your fishing rod in that old thing?"

"Just the fish," replied Maddox. He opened the latch of the suitcase. Inside was a bag of water with a knot at its top. An odd brown and orange fish about the size of a fist fluttered about inside.

"What is that?" said Chloe.

"It's a fish."

"That doesn't look like any fish I've ever seen," said Chloe. "Really, what are we doing?"

"Honestly, Miss Chloe, you do have a habit of repeating yourself," said Maddox, holding up the bag. "We're fishing."

Chloe looked closely at the creature swimming around in the cloudy water. Its face was wide, and it had a pronounced underbite of protruding teeth. A sharp fin rose from the top of its head and stretched nearly the length of its spotted body. Two fat flippers waved back and forth lazily.

"But you've already caught one," said Chloe.

"This is no ordinary fish," said Maddox. "It's a Billyfish."

"I have no idea what that is."

"The general public isn't aware of their existence," said Maddox. "They're also outlawed amongst us magicians."

"A strange thing to be outlawed," said Chloe, touching the bag with her finger. One of the Billyfish's eyeballs moved, and she drew away quickly.

"Billyfish are sensitive to magic. Extremely sensitive," said Maddox. "They can sense it from far away. Even distinguish between different types of potions and spells."

"How did you get one if it's outlawed?" said Chloe.

"Just because something is forbidden doesn't mean you can't get it," explained Maddox. "Everything is available for a price: every magician in London knows there's a man in Camden Passage who sells them."

"You still haven't said why people can't have them," said Chloe.

"Like I said, Billyfish are magic sensitive. They're addicted to it. Once one gets a whiff of magic, it can think of nothing else. It will stop at nothing to reach the source."

Maddox poked the bag gently, but the Billyfish didn't move. "These fish were once abundant in London's rivers. You can imagine the nuisance of having magic sensitive fish swimming in and out of London's realms, homing in on spells and then chasing after the magicians who cast them. Billyfish can survive out of water for long periods of time. There would be schools of them flipping and flopping about the streets, banging against people's doors and sneaking into their houses. Normal people started to catch on and it became dangerous for us magicians. Using a Billyfish became a way to sniff us out."

"What happens when a Billyfish catches up with the spell?" said Chloe. "Do they bite?"

"I don't know," said Maddox, examining the bag. "They do have some nasty-looking teeth, don't they?"

Chloe sighed. "How is this going to help us find out what happened to Ixworth?"

Maddox frowned. "I haven't really gotten that far yet," he said sadly. "I was hoping if I brought a Billyfish to the workshop, it might sniff out any strange magic. You know—something someone used to break into the shop. Something I'm not picking up on."

"It doesn't seem to want to do anything," said Chloe, looking at the Billyfish. "Is it asleep?"

Maddox sighed. "I suppose it was worth a shot," he said tiredly.

The two stood awkwardly staring at the odd fish in the bag.

Chloe thought for a moment.

"You said sniffed, right?"

"Sniffed?" said Maddox. "Oh! Right. Yes. The Billyfish sniffs for magic."

Chloe had an idea. She let it play out in her head before she spoke again.

"What is it?" said Maddox.

"My dad always burns his toast," said Chloe. "Do you know how annoying that is?"

"I can see how that could get on someone's nerves, but I don't see the meaning."

"He does it all the time," Chloe continued. "Mum will be making pancakes or baking a pie or something, and the delicious smell from those things will get ruined by my silly dad burning his toast."

"I still don't understand," said Maddox.

"Maybe you're the burnt toast," said Chloe looking at Maddox. "Didn't you say a magician's magic has a certain flavour to it? Maybe the Billyfish can't sniff out anything because all it can sense is you."

Maddox's eyes grew wide. "You know, Miss Chloe, that makes a lot of sense."

Chloe's idea bloomed further. Stepping away, she searched the abandoned shop. Beside the door the remains of a broken chair were propped lopsidedly against the wall. One of its spindled legs lay beside it on the floor. Taking the chair leg, she knelt down beside Maddox's suitcase and gently removed the bagged Billyfish. She looped the knotted end of the bag around the end of the chair leg. The finished contraption looked like a hobo's sack and stick.

"Now we really are fishing," said Maddox, clapping. "Absolutely brilliant, Chloe."

"You're going to need to keep out of the way or it's going to latch onto your smell," said Chloe, one hand steadying the bottom of the bag as she walked. When she reached the far end of the end of the workshop, she turned quickly, pivoting on one heel. "Ready?" she said, as she released her hand from the bag.

Maddox retreated well back from the entrance to the workshop as Chloe began to move back toward him.

Inside the bag, the Billyfish had come alive and was now swimming hard, swishing its tail and flopping clumsy flippers, pushing against the side of the bag, a drastic change from the lazy fish from a moment before. Chloe held her fishing rod aloft, letting the Billyfish guide her. She took a few unsteady steps, keeping the rod level as the Billfish led her forward. Clearly it was swimming toward the entrance of the workshop.

"I think it's found something," said Chloe.

"Evidently," said Maddox.

The Billyfish swam harder now, the target of the lazy-eyed fish becoming clear with each of Chloe's steps.

"The hat rack?" said Maddox.

Chloe stood a few paces back from the hat rack, ignoring the frantic swimming fish. "Maybe it didn't work," she said.

"No-no-no, I think it did," said Maddox, coming closer to examine it. "Something isn't right about this. But what's more puzzling is that I didn't realise it before. Even standing before it now, I'm getting nothing. All these times I've walked past it, even hung a coat upon one of the hooks. I never suspected."

Chloe unhooked the bagged Billyfish and stowed it back in Maddox's briefcase. She came to stand beside him.

"How could I have missed it?" said Maddox.

"It doesn't seem that special" said Chloe, approaching the hat rack.

"Don't touch it!" Maddox cried.

Chloe pulled her hand away. "Why?"

"Because I think somebody's been sneaking into the workshop," said Maddox. "And this hat rack is a doorway."

"Why do you think that?" said Chloe, watching Maddox sniff the hat rack as if it were the cork of an expensive wine.

"Please don't get too close," said Maddox, circling. "I doubt very much it works by contact, but I don't want to take any chances."

"But where does it go?" said Chloe.

"I wish I knew," said Maddox. "The more I think about this, the more it seems Ixworth was the victim of foul play. Somebody was here. Somebody neither of us knew about."

Chloe surveyed the empty space around them. "Do you think they were trying to steal something?"

"It's possible," said Maddox. "We do have some extraordinary rarities."

"Maybe Ixworth caught them in the act," said Chloe. "Or maybe he even found out about the hat rack and went through."

"Yes-yes-quite-right," said Maddox. "You make some good points." He turned suddenly, moving back toward the hat rack. "This is a very clever device. It's so discreet, so under my nose, so to speak. I would be hard-pressed to notice its use, even in my own realm."

"But that hat rack is yours, isn't it?" said Chloe.

"It is," said Maddox, scratching his beard. "I've had it for years.

"Where did you get it?" said Chloe.

"I bought it on a whim," said Maddox, "from a shop on Allen Street that was having a final closing sale." He stopped suddenly, a look of alarm on his face. "That's just off the high street in Kensington. Blythe's realm."

Chloe felt a hot flush of anger. "Blythe did this? He kidnapped Ixworth?"

"Let's not jump to conclusions just yet," said Maddox, furrowing his brow. "It may just be a coincidence. Blythe does have a motive. He's been after Ixworth's realm for years. But kidnapping seems a bit extreme, even for Blythe. Besides, didn't Ixworth say Blythe himself was missing? Wasn't his bodyguard looking for him here?"

Chloe recalled the tense exchange between Ixworth and the Block.

"Two missing magicians?" said Chloe.

"Three, actually," said Maddox. "There's an article in the Quarterly Crow—the issue that Ixworth was so obsessed with, remember? You read the headlines to me. It mentions a Mr. Brockwell missing from Wandsworth. Wandsworth is close to Thirsk's realm."

"So Thirsk is behind everything?" said Chloe. "He kidnapped Ixworth? And maybe Blythe too?"

"And is following you," said Maddox shaking his head.

"What does it all mean?" said Chloe, wondering if Maddox was as mixed up as she was.

"I haven't a clue," Maddox replied. "Really. Not the foggiest notion. But one thing is certain: this hat rack serves a purpose."

"If it's a doorway like you say, I think we should use

it," said Chloe. "We could just pop through and find out who's been using it. We might even find Ixworth on the other side."

"Absolutely not," said Maddox. "It's too dangerous."

"So you're just going to leave it sitting here?" said Chloe, pointing to the hat rack. "Knowing that someone could step through at any time? That doesn't sound very smart."

Maddox stared at the hat rack as if he were seeing it for the first time. "You make another good point. I shouldn't leave it unattended. I think I can conjure something sneaky that won't interfere with its workings but will alert us to its use. Perhaps I'll throw in an *Ebenezer's Mirror* for good measure. That will give me some time to think this through properly. I don't particularly like the idea of strangers in my shop. Anyone entering unannounced is going to have to answer for it."

CHAPTER 11

THRICE AROUND THE HAT RACK

"I want to try using the hat rack," said Chloe when she came into the shop the next day.

"I beg your pardon?" said Maddox from his spot behind the register.

"You need to show me how."

"Miss Chloe, we've already talked about this. It's too dangerous. What would your parents say if you got hurt? They'd report me to the police, I suspect."

"You can protect me," Chloe said. "Wasn't it you who said 'given enough time, people can prepare for anything'?"

"We don't even know what's on the other side," said Maddox tiredly. "If it's away from my realm, my magic won't have the same potency."

"But it still works, yes?"

Maddox nodded. "Of course."

Chloe thought for a moment. "What if we made a potion kit with the most annoying spells you can think of? I could carry some with me, and you could take some with you. Really sneaky spells like the one you made for Mr. Thirsk. We could jump through, find out where the hat rack goes and come back. It would only take a second."

"No-no-no," said Maddox, shaking his head.

Chloe approached the counter. "How else are we going to find out what happened to Ixworth? Or what that weird note in his pocket was all about?"

Maddox cleared his throat. "I don't know."

"Don't you want to figure it out?" said Chloe.

"You know I do," replied Maddox.

"I told you I wanted to help," Chloe continued. "You lost your best friend. You don't have to figure this out by yourself. I want to help."

Maddox was quiet for a moment. "You're quite a determined pupil," he said after a moment. "I'll consider it—but only consider. I could change my mind. I still think it's too dangerous."

While Maddox decided, Chloe spent the next two days hiding out in her room with the door closed, practising her *Rosebud*. She was feeling more confident. Each time she made one, it became easier. The next time she saw Maddox, she would ask his opinion. Perhaps he could start to show her how to add something to it properly.

Chloe was determined not to ask Maddox if he had reached a decision about using the hat rack. Thankfully, magic was on his mind when Chloe saw him that Sunday.

"Have you had any luck with the *Rosebud*?" he said

as soon as she came through the door.

Chloe raised an eyebrow. "I was just going to ask you to test me," she said. "I've been practising. A lot."

"Oho!" said Maddox. "Bravo. So, making progress, then?"

"I think I can make one every time I try," said Chloe shyly.

"Right," said Maddox. "Let's see."

Chloe went through the motions: Pinch thumb and forefinger, hands clockwise, counterclockwise, retention, spiderweb fingers. When she pulled her hands apart, a *Rosebud* remained in the palm of her hand, glowing like a tiny star.

Maddox was shocked. "Outstanding!" he said inspecting the glowing half-spell. He leaned in for a closer look. "Your retention is exemplary. Look at the colour—the sheen!" For a moment he stood quietly, looking at her. "You know. This could be very useful."

"How so?" said Chloe, feeling a little abashed from all the praise.

"You can help me," he said.

"With what?" said Chloe.

Maddox gave her a puzzled look. "Creating the potions we'll take with us around the hat rack, of course."

"Oh?" said Chloe.

Maddox waved his hand as if trying to shoo away Chloe's remark. "I have a few ideas already for your potion kit," he said, removing a wooden box from beneath the counter. It was lidless and divided into sixteen individual compartments. Several of them contained empty vials; others were filled with dried herbs. The compartments closest to Chloe held the bony-toed roots of several trees. "I was worried about potency," Maddox continued. "I'm not sure where the hat rack leads, but we're sure to be away from my realm. And you'll be using them. It would greatly enhance the potions if you contributed."

"I'm actually going to make my own potions?" said Chloe excitedly.

"Contribute," said Maddox. "Mind you, we'll need to be careful. Precision is key when two magicians create a spell together. One missed calculation and the magic can become uncontrollable. We want your potions to be stable. And of course, safe."

"What do I need to do?" said Chloe, trying not to seem too eager. They were, after all, doing something very serious in hopes of finding Ixworth.

Maddox took five of the vials from the wooden box and set them on the counter.

"Right, I'll need you to cast one of those brilliant *Rosebuds*—we'll use one for each of the five potions in your potion kit. I'll show you how I add the workings to the spell. You'll need to watch and study this part. We'll cover manipulating *Rosebuds* to serve a purpose during a future lesson. Time is of the essence."

"So, you've decided to use the hat rack? Like I said?" said Chloe.

Maddox gave Chloe a shy smile. "Miss Chloe, you had me convinced as soon as you suggested it."

Maddox disappeared to the rear of the shop but

was back a moment later with a thick mortar and pestle, the kind used to mash up herbs. Chloe had seen Mum use one to make guacamole a few months ago. She'd been urging Dad to try new things. Dad rudely made a retching noise, and the mortar and pestle went back into the cupboard. Experiment over.

Maddox prepared the ingredients while Chloe focused on the task of making her *Rosebuds*. She worked slowly, being careful to only use precise finger movements while focusing on each spell's retention. After spinning each one, she would let it drift gently over to Maddox, who would then take it in his palm and add a pinch from whatever he was mixing at the moment.

The process of casting spells was both harder and easier than Chloe had imagined. Harder because creating and maintaining five *Rosebuds* was exhausting. Easier because, in a way, magic seemed easy and natural to her. It was definitely not what she expected. Maddox didn't perform any rituals or chant hocus-pocus. Nor did he form any weird spinning disks in his hand. In three quarters of an hour, they had filled five tiny vials with magical potion. Chloe flexed her tired fingers while Maddox labelled each of the vials with a bit of masking tape. When he'd finished, Chloe took the one closest to her and examined the murky liquid inside. The label read *Uncle Albert*.

"What's this?" she said, feeling the weight of the vial in her hand.

"That, Miss Chloe, is something you and I made together," said Maddox. "These spells will be fine-tuned to you so you'll be able to use them properly and at full strength. That one in your hand is a disruption spell. It makes things go off kilter, float about, rise to the ceiling, move sideways, turn upside down. I've labelled all of the spells, lest you forget what each one does. Mind you, if you're in a pickle, I wouldn't pause to decide which to use."

"What should I use Uncle Albert for?" said Chloe, shaking the vial.

"It's all very innocent really," said Maddox, taking it gently from Chloe. "Say someone is trying to grab you. Use this. It will … well, let's just say I hope they have a fondness for ceiling fans if you know what I'm saying."

Chloe grinned. "How do I get it to work?"

"Just pop off the stopper," said Maddox, "or throw the vial. The secret is to put spells like this into fragile glass so they'll break easily, but be careful: they can work against you if you're too close."

Chloe picked up another vial. *Bubble-and-squeak.* "What's this one?"

"As it sounds, m'dear," said Maddox triumphantly. "Pop this off, and everything in the spell's radius will come together in a mash. People, furniture. Cats! You should avoid releasing it around liquids unless you're a good distance away. This attracts just about anything, and when liquids are involved, it makes a right mess."

Chloe nodded approvingly.

"Let me guess, this is a water potion of some kind," she said, pointing to a vial marked *River Thames.*

"Somewhere inside that head of yours is a magician waiting to come out," said Maddox proudly. "You're close. This is a fog potion, as the name might suggest, for Old Man Thames is the father of all fog. A night-full of London's thickest in one tiny bottle.

"The last two vials, *I'm-not-here*, and *Misplaced* need some explanation," he continued. "It's good you left these two until the end. They're by far the strongest. I would advise extreme caution when using them." He held *I'm-not-here* between his fingers. "If someone has you cornered—a person, a brownie, an elephant—drop this. It will give them partial amnesia. Like I said about the other potions, don't get too close to this when it comes alight, otherwise you'll be hanging about with your would-be attacker, wondering what the pair of you are doing."

Maddox packed all the vials back into the wooden box, leaving *Misplaced* on the countertop in front of him. "I think this is one of my favourite potions at the moment," he said excitedly.

"It's another memory spell, yes?" said Chloe.

"Correct, but a very particular memory spell. It gives one the overwhelming feeling they've forgotten something. So much so, they can't think about anything else and must immediately stop what they're doing to go find it."

"That is sneaky and horrible," said Chloe, looking at the vial. "I hate when I've lost something."

"As do I," said Maddox. He put the vial away with the others. "The spells are ready. Are you sure you're up for this?"

"Absolutely," said Chloe.

"No second thoughts?" said Maddox. "You know it could be dangerous?"

"It was my idea," said Chloe. "I want to do this."

Maddox examined Chloe, worry on his face. "If you're sure, we'll do it tomorrow. I have some spells of my own to prepare."

✦ ✦ ✦

Dad had once given Chloe his old waist bag. He had been weird about it, perhaps thinking it an heirloom of sorts, like a pocket watch or something to be passed along to his firstborn. Chloe had received the unfashionable belt like one being handed a raw fish. The waist bag had been left forgotten in her bottom drawer up until that Monday morning.

Chloe examined her reflection in the mirror: black leggings, plain grey t-shirt, denim jacket, her mobile bulging from the top pocket, pink trainers. Something was missing. She went to her top drawer to find her knitted tuque. Perfect. She attached Dad's waist bag, striking a pose.

Chloe walked briskly to the shop. Big bold steps. It felt good to be taking action. There was a chance this whole mystery would be cleared up by the end of the day. She and Maddox would use the hat rack. Ixworth would be found! He'd explain it was all just a mix-up: maybe he'd just been sick, or he'd needed to visit a friend out of town. All three would laugh about the silliness of it all.

Chloe's strides grew smaller as she neared the shop. Had it gotten hotter? The waist bag felt like it weighed ten stone and hung low on her waist, bulky and uncomfortable. What she was about to do had never been done by Mum nor Dad nor Iris—none of the kids in her school. Most people in London had never even considered travelling by hat rack.

"I've made tea," said Maddox as Chloe came through the door to the shop. "I thought you'd be feeling nervous. It's peppermint. It does wonders to temper my mood when I'm in one. Here, I'll pour."

Chloe came and stood beside Maddox. A china pot with two matching cups and saucers sat on the counter in front of him. Carefully, he measured out two cupfuls of tea and pushed a cup and saucer toward Chloe.

"You're not going to disappoint me if you decide not to do this. You're braver than most for even considering it."

Chloe sipped from her cup, breathing in the sweetness of the tea. "It does seem a little crazy," she said. "You have the spells?"

Maddox lifted the wooden box from the shelf beneath the counter. The vials inside clinked together happily.

"I have a waist bag," said Chloe.

"Oh?" said Maddox. "What are we wasting?"

"It's to carry the spells," said Chloe, running her hands along the outside of the bag like it was a championship belt.

Maddox nodded. "Seems a more practical way of

carrying glass vials," he said. "Mind they don't knock into each other and break."

"I'll be careful," Chloe replied.

Maddox patted his jacket pocket. "I've prepared a few things of my own." He looked at Chloe, and a worried moment passed between them.

Chloe struggled for something to say, gave up, and drained her cup instead. "Wouldn't want to waste the tea," she said. "I'm ready."

They took the lift to the basement. On the descent, the *hurumm hurumm* of the lift wheel sounded like the rumbling of a distant train. Chloe followed Maddox to the workshop, and they stopped an arm's length from the hat rack. It seemed such an ordinary thing. For the briefest of moments, Chloe wondered if they had made a mistake. Perhaps it was just as it appeared: a simple hat rack.

Maddox carefully set the box of spells beside Chloe and stepped away. Chloe stooped, removed the five vials and placed them in her waist bag. She zipped it closed.

"Now, what do we do?"

"I'll go first in case there's something unexpected on the other side," said Maddox. "When it's your turn, plant your hand firmly on the base of the hat rack." He pointed to a worn spot beneath the hooks. "The unpolished bit is probably from hands gripping and turning around. Magicians have a fondness for threes: one to start, two for good luck, and three just in case one has left the kettle at the boil or forgotten something. So three turns for you. Make sure you go all the way around for the third one, and be prepared for trouble. If something happens to me and you can't get back to the hat rack, use those spells. Don't be bothered by which, just keep your distance, and get back here if there's any trouble. Understood?"

"I'll be alright," said Chloe, checking to ensure the waist bag was tightly secured.

Maddox looked nervous. "If you see anyone, don't talk to them. Unless it's Ixworth, of course. We just want to find out who's been sneaking into the workshop."

"Does it matter which way I go around?" said Chloe, looking at the hat rack.

"Adding such a subtle rule would make the spell overly complicated, and really, what purpose would it serve?" said Maddox. "Now, ready?"

Maddox gripped the base of the hat rack firmly, and with a solemn look, began to turn. At the end of the third rotation, his body bent and contorted oddly, a puzzling arrangement of body parts. A cuff where a shoulder should be. A misplaced elbow. Then he seemed to just fold himself over and wink away into nothing. Gone.

Chloe took a deep breath. Stepping forward, she placed her hand on the base of the hat rack and began to turn. Once. Twice around. The cool metal was smooth in her grip. For a moment, she wondered if it was going to work the way it was supposed to, but then she suddenly experienced the oddest sensation she could remember having. The workshop, distorted by her turning, seemed to become a copy of itself. A mirrored reflection on still water. Then, like a swirling kaleidoscope, a place Chloe didn't recognize appeared over top of it. Chloe had left Maddox's workshop. She was now somewhere else.

CHAPTER 12

VOICES IN THE HALL

Chloe remembered taking a car trip to Portsmouth when she was small. Dad, perhaps driving faster than he should have around a slippery bend, had gone off the road. Nobody had been hurt, but she could still recall how she'd felt during the accident. The separation between herself and reality. The drag of time. Her last turn around the hat rack was like that.

People were not meant to travel by hat rack because it takes an eternity.

Chloe's arrival was a wobbly, off-kilter landing. It left her feeling like her body had been stretched out like an image in a carnival mirror. It was a long moment before she could gather herself and begin to take in her surroundings. Eventually, she realised she had left the workshop and was now standing in the cramped corner of a very untidy office.

Maddox was nowhere to be seen.

Chloe took a breath and tried to relax. Sneaking about looked so much easier in films. In real life, it was terrifying. The hat rack was beside her, a finger's length away. For a moment she was tempted to use it. Three whirls around and she would be back in the safety of the workshop. *I'm not a baby,* she thought. They had come to find Ixworth. She took a step forward, determined to finish what she had started.

It was clear Chloe had arrived in someone's house. Around her, all was quiet, save the settling of the foundations and the restless popping of pipes from behind walls. Somewhere distant, a clock ticked patiently. Chloe took note of the messy office. There were books on every surface: piled high on bookshelves, on an antique corner table, on chairs, on the floor, and stacked in corners. Several rolls of old parchment had been piled beside a desk that stood in front of a window. To her left, an assortment of vials containing vomit-coloured liquids was perched on top of a worn, dry sink. On the wall behind, someone had tacked up several photos of old theatre masks. But it was the map dotted with pushpins beside the photos that caught Chloe's attention. She leaned closer, noting the pins that had been arranged in an irregular line from Marylebone through Mayfair to Green Park. She took her mobile from her pocket and snapped a picture.

To her left, the office door stood ajar, showing a sliver of the dim hallway beyond. Chloe took three measured steps across the worn hardwood, thankful the soles of her trainers were soft and useful for creeping about. She hesitated at the door, taking a moment to listen. She was tempted to call out for Maddox. Why would he leave her alone in a strange house? Wasn't he the one who'd said this was going to be dangerous? She waited, but there was no sign of life. When she was sure it was safe, she peered out into the hallway. A flight of stairs rose to her left. At the top, the door to a bedroom stood open. Beyond the staircase, the hallway continued to two closed doors.

Summoning her courage, Chloe left the office, keeping close to the wall. On her right, a heavy wooden frame hung without a picture. Chloe fought the urge to run a finger along the dusty edge. She thought it best not to touch anything.

Chloe unzipped her waist bag and rummaged inside. The smooth glass of the vials rolled beneath her fingers. At the top of the staircase, she stopped. Below was a foyer with grey walls and a dull wainscotting. A spindly chandelier hung from above like a thin spider. In the corner beside the front door was another hat rack. A black steamer trunk had been placed near it as if set to be taken away.

Suddenly, she heard voices from below.

Chloe darted into the bedroom at the top of the staircase. It was tidy and well kept, a stark contrast to the office. A small bookshelf stood inside the door, stacked with old books and magazines. To the right, a narrow daybed sat in front of a window, a grey curtain partially drawn across. A tidy garden was just visible outside. A worn leather armchair was pulled close to a brick fireplace that still contained the ashes of a cold fire. But by far the most striking thing about the room was the other hat rack (three in one house!) nestled in the corner beside the chair. Chloe noted the uneven texture along the bottom of the hooks, which made it unlike the rack in the abandoned workshop. With few options, she squeezed in beside it, being careful not to touch the polished metal.

Two people were climbing the stairs. Their voices grew louder: one mild, the other high pitched and squeaky. As they neared, Chloe was able to snatch some of their muffled conversation.

"The boss is a tad worried about safeguards," said a mild voice.

"Oh," said a higher pitched voice. "On the premises?"

"Yes, here," said the milder voice. "Around his special guest too. But especially around the workshop entrance."

"Understood. It should already be undetectable, but we'll have someone go and add something extra to be safe."

"What can we do about the premises?" said the mild voice. "We don't want that magician showing up again?"

"We've already begun preparations," said the squeaky one. "We've cast *Pando* in the hedges in case someone tries to sneak through the garden. An airborne *Sporatica* to counter any *Levitations*. And I'll have a *Bushmat* sprinkled across the threshold for extra protection."

"Good idea. That should keep him at a distance for now."

Chloe removed one of the vials from her waist bag, holding it tight in her palm. *Uncle Albert* or *River Thames* seemed the most obvious choice given her situation, but she was too scared to move her eyes from the door to read the label.

"Was there any mention of some creature comforts to be taken across?" said the higher voice. "Furniture, perhaps?"

Chloe clutched the vial, ready to throw. There was a long pause, a sound like pacing footsteps.

"It's not on my list," said the mild voice. "The boss said he'll make do with the available furnishings. It's just a temporary move. Until he figures out what he's going to do with his house guest. We've collected a few personal possessions already. They're waiting to go across."

From her hiding place, Chloe tried to keep track of all the details. Somebody was taking precautions. Against whom, she didn't know. And what was that about the workshop entrance? The voices must have been talking about the hat rack. She had so much to tell Maddox. Where was he?

From the hallway, the footsteps renewed their rhythmic pacing, and the mild voice said, "Oh, yes. There was something else."

"Yes?" said the higher voice.

"The bodyguard. The boss has asked for someone to write him a note. Thank him, but say something's come up and his services won't be required for the next few weeks. It would be helpful if he stopped showing up at the house. He's scaring some of the others."

"I'll make sure it's done. Anything else?"

There was a long pause in the conversation, and for a moment, Chloe thought she might have been discovered.

"Oh yes," said the mild voice, "we've been asked to tidy the office."

"Oh?"

"It's an usual request," said the mild voice. "We're not usually asked to clean. Especially in his private space. It's quite unlike him to allow it to get in such a state."

"Shall we have a look now?"

The mild voice paused. "As long as we're quick. I'm due back soon."

The two speakers moved away, and the conversation continued out of earshot. Chloe waited until she was sure they had reached the office before moving out from behind the chair. She examined the label on the vial in her hand: *Bubble-and-squeak*. She carefully placed it back in the waist bag and made her way toward the stairs. Exiting through the front door seemed the only way to escape. She took a step, then stopped herself. One of the men had mentioned placing *Bushmat* across the threshold. Obviously it was an unfriendly spell to ward off unwanted visitors. Would it catch her on the way out? Before she could decide what to do, a brownie suddenly sauntered into the hallway with a bundle of books in its tiny hands. The brownie stopped, blinking in surprise. Chloe reached into the waist bag for a spell, reconsidered, thought of bolting down the stairs to the front door, but instead did something else. She darted back into the bedroom, squeezed in behind the chair, planted a hand firmly on the base of the hat rack, and then turned around. One turn, two turns—and she was off.

CHAPTER 13

HUSTINGS AND PUDDING

From the moment Chloe took her second turn around a hat rack, she knew something was wrong. She'd expected an uncomfortable journey, but the violent spinning she was experiencing at that moment felt different. Like a sickness creeping through her skin, leaking into her thoughts, muddling her sense of here, there, up, down, outward. As she swirled around in that terrible moment, she made a silent promise to never travel this way again.

This feeling came to an abrupt end when Chloe landed solidly on her back.

She might have been content to lie still, breathing in the relief one feels after narrowly escaping something terrible like a dog bite or drinking from a carton of sour milk. But the strangeness of where she had arrived forced her to sit up. She had landed on the lawn of a small park. A hat rack had been placed in the crook of a hedge just inside the park's entrance. It was different from the others she had seen: more slender, like a blackened tree, with curled hooks that ended in iron leaves. The thick base was set on a slab of dark stone and secured by heavy bolts. It was discreet enough to go unnoticed by those who passed it by.

Something was poking into Chloe's side.

Chloe turned. Two of Maddox's vials had shattered beneath her: *River Thames* and *I'm-not-here*. The open waist bag smiled wide, guilty of pending mischief. Chloe jumped to her feet.

River Thames suddenly erupted like a genie from a bottle, filling the air with a mushroom cloud of fog so dense and thick Chloe could feel it in her lungs. She stumbled a few feet, looking for a way to get out and away, glad the other vial, *I'm-not-here*, hadn't worked ...

What had she just been thinking about?

Chloe suddenly felt that she had awoken after a very long sleep. She was alive, standing up, and in a place that was difficult to describe. The air around her was billowing and ghost-like, yet she didn't know what it was nor how to describe it. She had no words and no memories. She had completely forgotten herself. Her name, the day of the week, where she lived, even the small things about herself. Was she a person? Did she like cucumbers? Why was this ugly thing strapped around her waist?

"I need to be away from here," thought Chloe, not in so many words, but more envisioning herself stumbling away from the place she was. She took a step forward, bumping into something tall with cragged skin and spindly arms that reached skyward. What was the name of it? A rush of rain-soaked air ignited a flash of memory. Chloe remembered a daybed in front of a window. A grey curtain. A feeling like falling upward. The memories faded, and she was back in the moment, staring out into a fenced park.

Fog continued to bloom up and out like a fat pudding, squeezing its doughy tendrils around trees and through shrubs. Chloe hurried away with clumsy stumbling steps, heading for a gap in the fence. Fog still clung to her clothing like discarded webs. Were people looking at her? She walked faster, brushing past the onlookers, and crossed a busy street. On the opposite pavement, she took a moment to catch her breath in the shadow of a building. The fog continued to rise.

Another showreel of memories flashed in her mind: Shopping for books. An old-fashioned elevator. Chloe fought a sudden urge to return to the park. Did she live there? So many things didn't make sense. She felt shivery pinpricks of panic rise up her back. Where was her family? Did she even have one?

A few people had stopped on the pavement not far from Chloe and were gaping at the park. Embarrassed, Chloe began to walk. She rounded a corner and came to rest in the shade of an overhanging tree. She didn't know where she was. She had no memory of the large town homes surrounding her. Several cars drove past— white, two red in row, black, black, blue, a little yellow one. Chloe realised some of her words were coming back.

"Excuse me," said someone from an expensive-looking old-fashioned car that had just pulled up beside her. The speaker was sitting in the back seat, his features hidden by the car's dark interior. "Miss? Are you all right?"

Chloe stared back dumbly.

"Can I help you?" said the man. "Offer you a ride home, perhaps?"

"I'm not quite sure where home is," said Chloe honestly.

The man considered this. "Come. We'll drive you. It's only a short way."

"How do you know where I live?" Chloe said suspiciously.

"I know a good many things, Miss Ashley," said the man.

"You know my name too?"

The silhouette of the man nodded.

"I don't know where I am," said Chloe. "Or who."

"Let me help you," said the man.

"I don't think I want your help," said Chloe, taking a step away from the curb.

"I think I would feel the same if I were in your position," said the man. "However, you seem to have suffered some ordeal. I would be negligent to leave you wandering these streets with no memory. You live in Mayfair, three minutes from this very spot. My driver and I will take you home."

Chloe couldn't decide which was worse: wandering the streets not knowing who she was or trusting this strange man.

"Clearly you've been befuddled by something," continued the man. "We're here to help. *You'll be fine.*"

Chloe suddenly felt as if she had been told an absolute truth. This man knew who she was. What harm would come by going with him? She took a step toward the car as a smartly-dressed man popped out of the driver's seat. In a flash he was around to Chloe's side of the car, opening the rear door and waving her to enter with a flourish of his hand.

"I'm Mr. Pudding," he said cheerily. "We'll take care of you, miss."

Chloe believed him through and through. He had such a kind face, one with deep crinkly smile lines. He offered a hand, and Chloe allowed him to help her into the car. The man in the rear had moved over, and Chloe climbed into the seat beside him. Mr. Pudding closed the door, shutting out the sounds from the road, and the car interior took on a heavy and serious tone like the air before a thunderstorm.

The man stretched out in the seat beside her was tall and dressed in a suit of dark grey with a matching tie. His face was difficult to see, for he seemed to wield the shadows inside the car, making them shift and dance to obscure his face. Only his piercing green eyes showed through.

The car began to move, and for a moment, Chloe felt hot with panic. She fumbled at the door handle.

"Miss Ashley," the tall man said, "no harm will come to you. I promise."

"Who are you?" said Chloe, turning toward him.

"Just someone interested in the order of things."

"I don't know how I got here," said Chloe trying her

best to blink back a head full of tears. "I was in a park full of ... fog! Or a cloud! It doesn't make any sense."

"I believe you've come under the influence of a potion," replied the man looking at her.

Chloe could see his mouth now, drawn thin with a slight smile. Did he have a beard? The rest of his face remained hidden. She couldn't put all the parts of it together into one complete picture.

"Perhaps it was something of your own doing?" said the man, pointing to the waist bag. "I believe there are other mischief-makers in that pouch you've got there."

Chloe glanced at the waist bag. The zipper was open, and three small vials sat inside. She removed one marked *Uncle Albert*.

"I would prefer if you didn't use that in here," said the man. "I have suspicion it wouldn't do either of us any good."

Chloe placed the *Uncle Albert* back in the waist bag and zipped it up. She suddenly remembered someone handing her the vials and the sound the little glass containers made as they clinked together.

"Do you recall how you came to arrive in this park of fog?" said the man.

Chloe shook her head. "No, sir." She was about to say something more but was struck by a rush of memories. She said them aloud as they came to her: "My name is Chloe Ashley. I have two friends, Ixworth and Maddox. My favourite thing in the world is reading good books." She leaned back in her seat, ashamed of her outburst.

"Seems to be coming back, then," said the man,

smiling wider. "Were your friends—this ... Ixworth and Maddox—the ones who gave you those potions?"

Chloe was afraid to answer, but it seemed rude not to. "I think so. Although. Are they potions? How can potions be real?"

"I think we both know potions are real," said the man pleasantly. "Seems an odd thing for you to be traipsing across London with a pouch-full of potions all by yourself."

Chloe suddenly felt woozy. The inside of the car began to spin. Then, another rush of memory flooded back in: her house, Maddox, Ixworth, the shop, all of the terrible business with Mr. Thirsk. The hat rack!

"Where are we?" Chloe said to the man beside her.

The man smiled. "Not where you intended to end up?"

Chloe tried to piece together events. Her travels had left her feeling apart from the world. "I don't know where I thought I'd end up," she said. "I've never travelled by hat rack before."

"Hat rack?" said the man, raising an eyebrow. "Why would someone travel by hat rack?"

Chloe suddenly wondered if she could trust this strange man. "I was looking for a friend," she said. "I got lost."

The man nodded, but his smile remained. They drove in silence, Mr. Pudding calmly navigating the car through the busy city traffic. Chloe turned to the window, watching mums and dads pushing strollers hung with shopping bags.

"This friend you were looking for," said the man after a few moments. "Was it Mr. Ixworth? I see you've come prepared with spells and whatnot. Perhaps to avoid trouble?"

Chloe wasn't sure if she should mention Ixworth's disappearance. It seemed unwise. Chloe stared back dumbly. The man—or the man's mouth—was smiling annoyingly. It was hard to tell if one belonged to the other.

"I haven't seen him for a few days," she lied. "I guess I was just messing about with something I probably shouldn't have been touching. I hope Maddox isn't mad."

"Just Maddox?" asked the man.

"No, no," said Chloe. "Ixworth and Maddox. I'm sure they're worried about me."

"I see," said the man. "And the potions you're carrying?"

Chloe tried to think of something to say.

"No harm-no harm," said the man, noting her discomfort. "This isn't a trial. Just making conversation. People carry around all sorts of things when they're out and about."

Chloe fell silent, knowing whatever she said, or didn't say, was revealing more than she wanted.

The car rounded a corner and slowed. "Oh, look: here we are, Miss Ashley," said the man. "Home again. Safe and sound."

Chloe studied the yellow brick home with tidy garden boxes. She recognized it as her own. "How do you know I live here?"

The man's thin smile was unwavering. For a

brief moment, Chloe was able to assemble his face into a complete picture. He was older than Ixworth or Maddox but not withered. Not greying. He was handsome, with sharp features and high cheekbones, a generous nose and a tidy head of dark hair. His movements were smooth and graceful. Chloe noted again the man's eyes. Like a cat's: all seeing and all knowing. Calculating and gathering every detail even from the backseat of his London car. He had the aura of a man in charge.

"It is my business to know all the affairs of this city," he said. "Small matters and large. Public and private. The going-ons of politicians and the comings-and-goings of citizens. And especially—especially—the conduct of its magicians."

Mr. Pudding opened Chloe's door and stood waiting patiently on the pavement.

"Take this," said the man beside Chloe. He handed her a business card:

Mr. Hustings, Alderman, London Proper.

There was a telephone number listed beneath his name.

"I'll be looking into this business with hat racks," said Mr. Hustings. "I don't think they're something that should be left lying around. A young lady might accidentally stumble upon one. End up transporting herself somewhere dangerous."

Chloe climbed from the backseat. From the

pavement, she thanked Mr. Hustings and Mr. Pudding for the ride.

"Please call if you need anything," said Mr. Hustings from the car window. "I'm available at all hours. Oh, and I hope you find your missing friend. Mr. Ixworth's always been good in my book."

Chloe watched the car pull away slowly, cruising to the end of the street and then turning out of sight.

Chloe checked her mobile: It was 13:22. She had been away from the shop for over an hour. She suddenly remembered Maddox was still missing. On a whim she telephoned the shop. Maddox answered immediately.

"What happened to you?" said Chloe.

"Miss Chloe! Thank heaven you're safe," cried Maddox in his scratchy land-line voice. "I've been worried sick!"

"Why didn't you come around the hat rack with me?" said Chloe. "Where did you go?"

"I tried," said Maddox, suddenly exploding into a fit of coughing. "I never made it through. I was tossed and turned between here and there for the longest time, then spat back out in the workshop. It seems to be some variation of an *Eviction,* I suspect. But enough about that—what happened to you?"

"It's hard to explain," Chloe said wearily. "I'm feeling wonky from travelling around all those hat racks."

"Hat racks?" said Maddox, trying to suppress more coughing. "Wait. There was more than one?"

"It's complicated," sighed Chloe.

"Complicated?" said Maddox. "What does that

mean? Are you safe? Please tell me you didn't get hurt."

Chloe attempted to recount her journey around the hat rack, but Maddox kept interrupting. "Listen Maddox, everything's fine," she said, tiredly. "I'm home now. Nothing happened."

"We're never trying something like this again!" Maddox bawled in reply. "You need to start again from the beginning. Tell me everything."

"I will," said Chloe, "but tomorrow. It feels like I've been gone for a week."

The line was silent for a moment. "Agreed," Maddox said finally, "but you need to come 'round the shop early. We have much to discuss."

* * *

"Now, to the order at hand," said Maddox, addressing Chloe after she arrived at the shop the next day. "I want to hear everything about your journey—from the moment you left to the time you got home."

Chloe recounted her story while Maddox listened, stopping her only when he needed something clarified or missed a detail. When she finished, Mr. Winch brought through a tray with a tea in fine china with clotted cream and fresh scones with jam.

"Who is Mr. Hustings?" said Chloe, taking her cup.

Maddox poured milk. "Mr. Hustings is the city Alderman. Think of him as the head magician," said Maddox.

"You've never mentioned him before," said Chloe.

"I suppose I've never had reason to," said Maddox mildly.

"But he knew who I was," said Chloe. "I can't believe I got into his car. A complete stranger! What was I thinking?"

"There's no need for alarm," said Maddox. "Mr. Hustings is not a bad man by any means. Although it seems quite the coincidence he was driving by when you were in distress. That is cause for concern."

"You don't think he's following me too, do you?" said Chloe.

"Not you specifically," Maddox said soberly. "You told Mr. Hustings you hadn't seen Ixworth for a few days, correct?"

Chloe looked down into her lap. "I'm sorry, Maddox. I just didn't know what to say. I just blurted it out. That bit about the hat racks too."

"It's not your fault," said Maddox. "He would have found out sooner or later anyway. Most likely he's looking into Mr. Blythe's disappearance. A missing magician means one of London's realms is sitting vacant. Other magicians may be wondering about that. Empty realms eventually get redistributed." Maddox paused for a moment thinking. "There are just so many unanswered questions. So many mysteries. Ixworth's disappearance. Mr. Thirsk skulking about. Now Mr. Hustings looking into things. It's very odd."

"Does Mr. Hustings usually check up on people?" said Chloe.

"He's not the policing sort, if that's what you're

asking," said Maddox. "His duties are for the benefit and good of all of London's magicians."

"Wait," said Chloe, "so there's a magician's club?"

"Yes," replied Maddox. "If you're a magician, you belong to the Magician's Guild. It's an association with rules and regulations to keep the peace. Otherwise we'd all be fighting and squabbling over realms. Like we used to."

"Magicians used to fight one another?" said Chloe.

"There is always fighting when power is to be gained," Maddox said sadly. "Remember, the larger a magician's realm, the more potential they have. There are exceptions, of course, but that is the general rule. In days gone by, one needed to be careful. Another magician might move into your realm and attempt to pinch it from you. As I may have mentioned, magicians hold no special bond to one another. The nature of our magic makes us adversaries."

They both stood silently at the counter for a long minute. The shop's cheery interior seemed suddenly diminished.

"I feel like I've messed everything up," Chloe said gloomily. "What if Mr. Hustings finds out how long Ixworth has been gone and gives away his realm?"

"It hasn't come to that yet," said Maddox. "But time is running out. We need to find out what happened to Ixworth—and soon."

"I think I wrecked our chance at that too," said Chloe.

"What do you mean?" said Maddox.

"I didn't find anything when I went around the hat rack," said Chloe. "Remember what I told you about the voices? About how they were going to add more protection to the entrance from the shop? There's no way we'll be able to go back around now."

"You're being a bit hard on yourself," Maddox said gently. He paused for a moment. "And actually, you have given us several clues."

"I don't think I have," said Chloe.

Maddox began pacing in front of the counter. "You overheard a conversation before you left this strange house. Did you recognize any of the voices?"

"No," said Chloe, shaking her head. "One kind of calm, the other happier, like—excited. They kept talking about their boss. I figure they were brownies because I saw one just before I used the second hat rack."

"And no mention of where they were going?" said Maddox.

"Just something about a house guest—and the bodyguard."

Maddox stopped his pacing. "Yes, the bodyguard. Blythe has a bodyguard. I think it's safe to assume they're talking about a move to or from his house."

"I was thinking the same thing," said Chloe.

Maddox was pacing anew, furiously now, from the counter to the front window display and back, fingers planted firmly on chin. "It would be helpful if we knew whose house you arrived in. Then we would know who's behind all of this. Any chance you remember any details?"

Chloe shook her head. "Just an ordinary house.

Maybe a little dusty. I think I was too scared to notice anything, really. Besides the stuff in the office."

"And what about that?" said Maddox looking at her. "Anything out of the ordinary. Odd looking books? Writings. Magical items?"

"Nothing that jumps out," said Chloe sadly. "It was all so strange. And messy. There were books and papers scattered everywhere. On the desk. On the floor."

"Anything else?"

Chloe thought for a moment. "Pictures of old masks?"

"What kind of masks?" said Maddox.

"Theatre masks, I think," said Chloe. "I remember learning something about them in school. But there was nothing exciting about them. I only remember because it was the only picture in the entire office."

"That's not much to go on," said Maddox. "It could mean something or nothing."

"There is something else," said Chloe, remembering. "There was a map of London tacked to the wall. Somebody had marked it with push pins. Here—look. I took a picture."

Chloe removed her mobile from her pocket and scrolled to find the picture. She showed Maddox.

"Too bad it's so small," he said, putting his nose to the screen.

Chloe pinched her fingers, enlarging a portion of the map.

"Oh! How clever!" cried Maddox. He looked closely. "Now, isn't that odd?"

"What?" said Chloe.

"Those pins are marking locations in my realm," said Maddox.

"I didn't understand it either," said Chloe. "It looks like the world map we have at school. People are allowed to mark where they've travelled or gone on holiday."

Maddox squinted again at the map. "This seems to be marking a route. Duke Street to Buckingham Palace, ending at the Thames."

"Do you think it means something?" asked Chloe.

Maddox scratched at his chin. "I don't know. You mentioned there was another hat rack in the park. Its proximity to your home suggests it's in Grosvenor Square. Two hat racks within my realm? Perhaps that's how Mr. Thirsk is sneaking about without being detected. I'll need to go find it. Perhaps place a counter spell to stop any unwanted intrusions. But there's something more pressing. Those brownies mentioned a house guest. Maybe that was just a polite way of saying prisoner. I think we should start looking for Ixworth at Blythe's residence."

"Do you know where he lives?" said Chloe.

"The address is on file," said Maddox. "Mr. Winch organised the delivery of his purchases."

"But it's sure to be guarded," said Chloe.

"You leave that up to me," said Maddox. "In the meantime, is there a way you can get me a more solid version of the map you have on that magical device of yours?"

CHAPTER 14

LIGHTNING

A taxi pulled up a few doors down from Chloe's house a little after two on Wednesday. Maddox leaned his head out of the rear window, waved and popped open the door. Chloe hurried to climb in beside him as it began to rain.

"I don't think I've ever seen you in a car," she said.

Maddox smirked. "I'll admit it's not something I'm used to," he said, running a hand over the worn seat. "I would much rather walk or," he lowered his voice, "use a bit of magic. But we don't want to draw attention to ourselves."

"Are you sure you know how to pay the driver?" Chloe teased, sensing Maddox's discomfort. "I can lend you some money."

"My shop does accept modern forms of currency, Miss Chloe," Maddox said dryly. "I know how to use money."

The taxi driver dropped them off at the end of Addison Road. Chloe and Maddox watched the car drive off as the spattering of raindrops turned to drizzle. The sky to the north of the city had grown dark and threatening, giving the afternoon a shade of early evening. They walked a short distance, stopping in front of the gate to a large house. It was three stories, each lined with windows, some arched, others flat. The entire bottom floor seemed to be constructed of white marble. The other levels were in a tanned well-to-do brick. A fire-engine-red door stood guarding the house.

"This is Blythe's house?" said Chloe.

"Pretentious, wouldn't you say?" said Maddox.

"If that means very showy, then yes," said Chloe, staring at the house for a long moment. She suddenly wondered who was locked up in the house. It seemed odd Blythe would be a prisoner in his own home.

"Mr. Hustings gave me his business card," said Chloe. "Should we call him? He could help us find Ixworth. Then we wouldn't need to worry about his realm being given away."

"I think we should leave Mr. Hustings out of this," said Maddox stiffly. "What you say makes some sense. And I would welcome his help. But what if Ixworth isn't here? Husting will be alerted to his absence and then we run the risk of speeding up his investigations. There's a chance someone is deliberately keeping magicians away from their realms, knowing the Alderman will need to look into it."

Chloe nodded and turned to examine the door to the house. "Have you figured out how we're going to get inside?" she asked. "Somebody's got to be home."

Maddox tutted. "You think you'd be used to chumming around with a magician by now. The matter is taken care of."

"Invisibility spell?" said Chloe.

"Come now," said Maddox. "Invisibility spell? Rubbish. You've been reading too many storybooks. Need I remind you, this is the real world."

"So how do we get in without being seen?"

Maddox opened the gate, letting Chloe through. They walked casually up to the front door like they were dropping in for tea.

"Ever since I was *Evicted* from Ixworth's realm, I've been working on some spells. Spells to help me get around once I broke the *Eviction*. Whoever cast it made it strong, for it has foiled every attempt I've made to crack it. However, this is Holland Park. It's not protected in the same way, so these little gems will do just fine."

"No more hat racks, I hope," said Chloe.

"Of course not, m'dear," said Maddox. "Two spells I have yet to name. They're a little unconventional, but then again, a lack of convention is the difference between a good magician and a great one." Maddox produced two objects from his jacket pocket: an antique brass door knocker and a child's winter boot.

"I have no idea how those are going to help us," said Chloe.

"I'll explain," said Maddox. "It helps if the spell is focused on an object. It makes the magic easier to manage. For me anyway. These objects have some symbolic value as well, which is useful."

"I'm scared," said Chloe.

"There's no need to worry," Maddox said gently. "Now quick, behind me."

Chloe moved behind Maddox.

"Grab a corner of my coat," he said, turning his head, "and don't let go. I don't want you being left behind. Quickly now. Got it? Good. Now ready?"

Maddox held the brass knocker to the door with one hand, and with the other, knocked once. Chloe had a sudden sensation of spinning, round and round, in small tight circles. She shut her eyes. Maddox sounded the knocker once more and the feeling stopped.

When Chloe opened her eyes, they were standing in the front foyer of a posh house. Maddox was beside her. He dropped the child's boot. It landed softly on the tiled floor and turned on its side. There was a noise—*wump*—a deep swelling whale-call of a sound. Chloe felt the world lurch to the left. She fought the urge to wretch.

"You all right?" said Maddox, resting a hand on her shoulder.

"What was that?" said Chloe.

"Just a little thing I cooked up," said Maddox.

Chloe hunched over her knees, taking several deep breaths. "Does magic always make a person feel sick? That felt like ten turns around the hat rack."

Maddox thought carefully. "It's normal for one to feel a little off after being *Displaced*. Give it a moment."

Chloe stretched, trying to shake off the sense of spinning. "Shouldn't we be whispering?"

"Whispering?" said Maddox

"You're talking loud for a person that's just snuck into a house. Someone's going to hear us."

"Oh," said Maddox, unbuttoning his coat and removing a bit of stray lint that had found its way beneath the lapels, "we don't need to worry about that. The boot took care of it."

"The boot?" said Chloe.

"I'm thinking of calling it an *Unusual Juxtaposition*, or a *Brief-Moment-Left*. Which do you like?"

"I have no idea what you're talking about," said Chloe, having recovered somewhat from the effects of the spell. She stared at the boot sitting just inside the door. "It's not an invisibility spell, then?"

Maddox was casting an eye to the rich furnishings of the foyer, "No. But let me assure you, we're safe. No one is going to be able to detect us. Not really, anyway. If anything, they might think we're ghosts that have taken up residence in this ..." he paused to consider, "... mansion."

Maddox walked to the middle of the foyer, spreading his arms wide as if drawing the details of the house inward. "A lesson for you, Chloe, seeing as you're well on your way to becoming a magician. Magic is not simple or ordinary. Ever. Well, never say never, but sometimes—most of the time—it's unordinary. A person might be inclined to be practical. As an example: breaking into a house, like we did today, using an opening charm seems logical, correct?"

Chloe shrugged, thinking hard. "I think my spell casting is a little different than yours, but I think I know what you're saying."

Maddox continued, "Most magicians can

deconstruct an opening charm without even thinking about it. They'll even put up counter spells to prevent them. Remember what I said? A magician needs to be creative. The *Inside-Outside* door knocker I just used charmed the front entrance into believing—yes, doors do have minds of their own—that it was keeping the outside in, and should really be keeping the inside out, allowing us to enter the house without any trouble."

"That makes no sense at all," said Chloe, shaking her head.

Maddox raised an eyebrow. "That device you have with you all the time, that *mobile,* do you think that makes any sense? Calling people from all over the city. Typing your little alphabets into the screen? All those little willy-whoops and wizzle noises. Honestly."

Maddox wandered the foyer, examining the artwork on the walls like he had paid admission to a museum. He stopped just outside the entryway to a large dining area.

"Oho? Look what I found!"

Chloe came up beside him to see. A large table stretched the length of the room. A party of twelve chairs crowded around, waiting for their respective guests. Tucked in the corner beside the arrangement was a hat rack: heavyset with thick legs and a trunk that bore the likeness of city streets.

"Odd place for a hat rack," said Maddox, being careful not to touch it. "I wonder how many of these are scattered across the city?"

"That looks like the one Mr. Blythe bought from your shop," said Chloe.

"Yes," said Maddox. "And this is my point. I wonder what it means?"

"It seems a bit wonky Blythe bought a hat rack from you, and at the same time someone has been using another to sneak in and out of the workshop," said Chloe.

Maddox scratched at his beard. "Somebody really likes hat racks."

Chloe suddenly noticed something out of the corner of her eye: Movement from the far end of the foyer.

"Brownies!" she hissed.

Maddox noted their approach with disinterest. "Like I said, Miss Chloe. They can't hear us. Not properly, anyway. Just don't touch them. That might make them suspicious."

Chloe moved closer to the wall, giving the brownies room to pass.

"I'm not daft," said Chloe, watching the two brownies climb the staircase to the upper floor. "How does your spell work again?"

"*A Brief-Moment-Left?*"

"If that's what you've decided to call it."

"Simple," said Maddox. "You and I are here but just a little to the left."

"Say that again," said Chloe. "Left?"

"Left of here. Left of right now," said Maddox. "People outside the spell will just miss us by a hair's width."

"Time travel?" said Chloe.

"Time travel is impossible," said Maddox with a

hint of disgust. "This is something different. You and I, we're under the influence of the spell and are sharing a moment with those who are not. But just to the left."

For a second, Chloe thought she understood. But then the idea got muddled up in her head and she was back where she started. There were times when magic seemed impossible to work out logically. It was such a backward way of thinking.

Maddox led them away from the foyer, passing through a wide archway into a pantry. Farther ahead was a large kitchen. The smell of baking gave the room a warm and homey feel. Coming toward them was another twosome of brownies, one carrying a tray of small sandwiches, the other a tea service.

"It seems so crazy they can't see us," Chloe breathed after the two had passed. "You didn't happen to recognize any of them, did you?"

"What do you mean?" said Maddox, opening one of the pantry cupboards. Oh, look! Shortbread cookies."

"The brownies we just passed. They all look so alike. Do they work for Mr. Blythe?"

"Many magicians have brownies," said Maddox distractedly.

"It's like they just appear out of thin air."

"That's the thing about brownies," nodded Maddox, moving toward the far end of the pantry, "they have such a way of getting around: crawling between cracks, through tunnels. They have such a talent for sneaking about. Wondrous explorers too."

Chloe walked a few steps ahead of Maddox while he

searched the pantry. She stopped beside a large window that overlooked the garden.

"What? Is? That?" she said, motioning to a small ivory greenhouse with silver flourishes that sat on the wide windowsill. A lone plant grew within: bulbous, with thick spotted leaves and six spider-leg-like tendrils sprouting from its centre.

Maddox turned.

"Oh?" he said. "We sold that greenhouse to Blythe, if you remember." He approached and tapped on the glass roof.

Chloe winced at the sight of the plant growing inside. "That looks disgusting."

"Yes, they do look particularly nasty, don't they?" said Maddox.

"What is it?" said Chloe.

Maddox pressed his nose to the glass. "You are looking at a *Charmian Cabbage*. Probably the rarest plant there is. They're extremely hard to grow and only come from one place. In fact, I didn't think they could live outside their native Magdalen Islands. Something about the pull of the tides and whatnot."

"Do you eat them?" said Chloe, standing well clear of the greenhouse.

"Heavens no," said Maddox. "They're extremely dangerous. Devious too, as plants often are. Their poison is difficult to detect, and the symptoms of exposure differ so wildly. Lumps, piles, blots, rot, purple spots beneath the tongue, ear retching, Thad disease, armpit glumps, dry mouth."

"Why am I not surprised Mr. Blythe has one growing in his house?" tutted Chloe. "What does he need it for?"

Maddox stared through the glass for a moment longer. "I would suspect nothing good. Come on, let's keep looking. We came here to find Ixworth."

Chloe and Maddox searched the remainder of the ground floor but found nothing of significance and no sign of the mysterious house guest. Discouraged, they returned to the foyer where the sound of rain was heavy on the walls and windows.

"We should have brought umbrellas," said Chloe.

Maddox was lingering near the window beside the front door. "Indeed … Oh! Look at this!"

Chloe came up beside him. "What are you looking at?"

"There's somebody outside."

Chloe peered out into the gloom. There was a figure standing in the rain, their back to the gate.

"Who is it?" said Chloe

"Blythe, I should think," said Maddox. "But I can't be certain."

The figure turned suddenly, heading toward the house.

"Best we move out of the way," said Maddox, leading Chloe away from the door toward the darkened dining area. "We'll watch from over here."

There was a brief moment when it seemed the mysterious figure had gone away, deciding instead not to enter, but then the front door flew open amidst a flurry of rain drops. Someone dressed in a short coat stood on the threshold, face hidden by a high collar and hood. The figure turned away abruptly, exiting back into the rain, leaving the door to swing wildly.

Maddox crept toward the door.

"Where are you going?" Chloe hissed.

"I need to find out who it is," said Maddox.

"Don't leave me here!" cried Chloe, hurrying after him.

They crossed the foyer to the door. Beyond, the streets were awash in sheets of rain. The hooded stranger had moved just beyond the gate and was watching someone approach from the road: a tall slender frame wrapped haphazardly in a flapping coat.

"Good heavens!" Maddox exclaimed. "I think that's Mr. Thirsk."

"Which one?" said Chloe.

"The farthest one. The one on the road."

"How do you know?" said Chloe.

Maddox turned to Chloe, raising an eyebrow. "Long coat. Frame like a rake. Frazzled crazy hair. Hat. Do you know anyone else who looks like that?"

"Who's the other one? The one in the hood?"

Maddox turned back to watch. "I haven't a clue. Let's keep watching."

Mr. Thirsk had stopped several metres from the gate. The other figure was shouting angrily, their words drowned out by the rain. Thirsk looked on, unimpressed.

"Is this a meeting?" said Chloe, feeling a sudden

sting from Ixworth's absence. "It figures Thirsk would be involved in some way."

"I don't think this is a friendly get-together," said Maddox.

"It's not?" said Chloe.

Maddox's eyes were locked on the events unfolding on the street. "Something is happening here. Look!"

A bloom of intense light erupted from the gate with a thunderous roar. When it subsided, Mr. Thirsk was lying on his back several yards from where he had been standing. His weathered overcoat was smouldering. Something powerful had knocked him down. For a moment, he appeared dead, but then he roused, getting up slowly, climbing shakily to his feet. His grin—that mixed expression of glee and grim that Chloe remembered so vividly—was gone.

The figure by the gate was standing with hands clenched at their sides. Mr. Thirsk advanced toward the house, left leg dragging. He brought his hands up flat, palms forward, moving them sideways back and forth, like he was shaping the air. Something came alive in his hands, a spinning churning fire.

The hooded figure stepped forward to meet his advance. The air around them charged with ribbons of light, fanning out like eels of electricity. The hooded figure raised their arms, pulling upward, as if drawing a great weight. When they levelled their hands toward the advancing Mr. Thirsk, the street erupted again in a blast of blue fire.

"We need to get away from here!" Maddox winced

above the echo of the second blast. "We're in danger if we stay!" He grabbed Chloe by the arm, pulling her away from the door.

"What type of magic is that, Maddox?" Chloe said shakily.

"I don't know," said Maddox. "This is beyond anything I know. Anything I thought possible. The strength of these magical exchanges is weakening everything around them. My *Brief-Moment-Left* is going to collapse unless we get away from this house. It just can't hold up to this type of punishment."

They fled toward the rear of the house amidst a rush of brownies who had come to investigate the disturbance. A few of them gave Chloe puzzled looks as they flew past. As they rounded the corner coming into the pantry, a brownie collided with Chloe, and she stumbled.

Maddox steadied her. Several of the brownies had stopped and were looking at them with cautious interest.

"Maddox!" Chloe cried. "They can see us! The spell has stopped working!"

Maddox reached into his jacket and drew a vial from the inside pocket.

"Just be ready to run when I say," he said, preparing to throw.

The brownies suddenly stopped, confused by the sputtering and starting of Maddox's spell. Another detonation thundered from the front of the house. Maddox grabbed Chloe by the wrist pulling her away.

"Off we go," he said, heading for the nearby staircase.

"We've moved left again. Hurry! The spell is almost expired. We only have a few seconds before it's gone for good. If we're quick, we might just give them the slip."

"We're going up?" Chloe cried, footsteps fumbling as she tried to keep up with Maddox. "How is that going to help us get out?"

"If you can think of a better option," Maddox huffed, "I'm ready to hear it. Besides, I can't imagine we'll ever be able to set foot in this house again with all that's happened. We may discover a clue. Now, quickly! Before those brownies come after us!"

The top of the house was split into two landings, one on either side of the staircase. Two doors right, two left. A single door stood in the middle. Chloe kept close to Maddox, fearing she would be left behind. Maddox threw open the first door, revealing an empty guest room. There seemed no way to escape, save through the window and down to the street below. He turned quickly, heading toward the second door. When he realised it was a lavatory he moved on, stopping when he reached the last door.

"Pray for luck," he said, turning the handle. The door opened to another guest room. A large window overlooked a garden of old trees and a wall. The greenery of Holland Park stood in the distance.

"What do you want?" someone wheezed.

Maddox jumped back, startled by an elderly man who was sitting in an armchair in the corner of the room. A tray with tea and several untouched sandwiches sat on a small pedestal table beside him.

"Excuse us," flustered Maddox, "so sorry. Our mistake."

"Wait!" cried the man. "You—Maddox! and—girl. I know you," he said, pointing a bony finger.

"I don't believe you do," said Maddox, exchanging puzzled looks with Chloe.

"I need your help," the man said, attempting to climb from the chair. He teetered precariously on withered limbs before collapsing back down.

"Have we met?" said Maddox.

"Yes," said the man, "I used to frequent your shop."

"Oh?" said Maddox, moving closer. "I don't think I recognize you. What's your name?"

The man coughed dryly. "You don't know?"

"Should I?" said Maddox.

"Of course you should. It's me, Blythe."

CHAPTER 15

INTO THE PARK

"Good heavens!" cried Maddox. "What happened to you?"

Mr. Blythe coughed. "Open your eyes," he wheezed. "I'm old."

"Yes, I can see that," said Maddox. "How?"

Mr. Blythe glanced at Chloe, who was still standing inside the doorway. "Why are the two of you in my house?"

"Searching for you, in a way," answered Maddox.

Mr. Blythe scoffed. "You've probably come to rob me."

"Rob you?" said Maddox.

"Yes," said Mr. Blythe. "You found out about my condition and have come to take advantage of me."

"I'm afraid I don't know what you're talking about," said Maddox.

They all stopped as another blast erupted from outside. Mr. Blythe looked uneasy, as if he knew the extent of the magic at work. "So you weren't aware?" he said cautiously.

"If you're referring to your altered appearance," said

Maddox, "then no. We've come for answers. There have been a number of very peculiar happenings of late."

"More peculiar than what I've suffered?" spat Mr. Blythe. He watched them for a long moment. "I don't know if I trust you, Maddox. But seeing as I have little option. Girl! Best you shut the door, otherwise we'll be discovered, and then who knows what will happen to you?"

Chloe poked her head out into the hallway to ensure they hadn't been followed. The last blast from the street had incited a ruckus of chattering from the brownies on the first floor and seemingly had sent them all scuttling for the front of the house.

"I think we're okay for the moment," she said, pulling the door shut.

"We haven't much time," said Maddox. "Someone is sparring with Mr. Thirsk outside. I have never seen anything like it in all my years as a magician."

"I don't suppose you have," said Mr. Blythe. He went into another fit of coughing, and it was a moment before he regained his composure. "My captor is twice the magician you are."

"It would seem," said Maddox, looking at him. "I have many questions about that, but first, who is it?"

Mr. Blythe shrugged. "Your guess is as good as mine. He and I are not on the friendliest of terms. I've never spoken to him." He paused, looking down at his hands.

"He did this to you?" said Chloe. Mr. Blythe's face was a roadmap of deep wrinkles, a withered apple beneath weeds of hair gone white. When he managed to move, he did so with difficulty, as if his gnarled limbs ran the risk of snapping from his hunched trunk. He was the oldest person she had ever seen.

"Yes," said Mr. Blythe.

"I don't know what to say," said Maddox. "Was it a potion? Some variation of a *Cupid's Deception?*"

"Not a potion," said Mr. Blythe, "nor a spell. An object. Like a mask."

Maddox shot Chloe a look.

"Did you happen to see what this mask looked like?" he asked Mr. Blythe.

"I wish I knew," said Mr. Blythe. "I didn't see it."

Maddox moved toward Mr. Blythe, waving a hand in front of his face.

"What are you doing?" Mr. Blythe said irritably.

"I was thinking your condition might be some clever illusion," said Maddox, "one that even fools its victim."

"Stop being ridiculous," snapped Mr. Blythe. "You think this is some trick and I've fallen for it like a fool? I can feel the old. In my hands and my bones. In my mind. My life has been stolen away."

"Right-right, I apologise," said Maddox. "We can help you. Tell me exactly what happened."

The din from outside had stopped, diminishing to a sprinkle of quiet raindrops on the window. As if taking comfort in this detail, Mr. Blythe sighed heavily, leaning his head against the back of his chair. When he spoke, his eyes were closed.

"It's all a little muddy. I only remember bits and pieces as if it happened in a dream. I had just sat down to a fine Moroccan lamb when someone showed up. Uninvited. I don't even know how they managed to get in the house. I have quite a vicious *Rosencrantz* surrounding the property. It is a marvel you managed to get in, Maddox. It's far stronger than anything you could ever decipher."

Maddox took this slight with grace. "I sensed no such spell when we arrived," he said mildly.

Mr. Blythe coughed. "Regardless, you can imagine my surprise when I was attacked in my own home. Before I even knew what was happening, I was befuddled by some kind of *palsy*. The coward! I had no time to react, otherwise ... well, they should consider themselves lucky."

"A *palsy*?" said Maddox. "I thought you said it was a mask that turned you old?"

"I'm not finished," said Mr. Blythe. "I was blindfolded and trundled off to who knows where. It was quite a dizzying experience. Through a maze or corridors. Down steps." He stopped suddenly, listening. Voices from the floor below were babbling excitedly.

Maddox reached inside his coat, pulling a small glass vile from the inside pocket. He loosened the stopper, keeping the vial in his palm. He looked at Mr. Blythe.

"The mask you mentioned, can you explain what happened?"

Mr. Blythe pulled himself higher in his chair. "I'll try." But he remained silent for a moment, his old brain churning with effort. "I was taken to a large space—you know how you can get a sense of a place by the echos?

It was like a dungeon or the tunnels beneath Waterloo Station. There was water close by, for I thought I could hear the rush of a waterfall, at least for some of the time." Mr. Blythe touched his arm. "This arm was bound in a clamp or device of some kind." He took a moment to swallow, highlighting the snake-like skin above his collar. "I asked my captor what he wanted—implored him to let me go—but he didn't say a word. I honestly thought he was going to kill me. But then something was placed over my face, I assume it was a mask, for it had been shaped and sat snug. I can still remember the terrible feeling while wearing it. Like I was drowning. It was only on for a moment, but it felt like a lifetime. And when it was finally removed, I felt like I had lost something. Like I had been drained away. I know it all sounds like madness. I don't believe it myself, but look at me."

"Was it immediately after this mask had been removed that you realised you had lost your youth?" Maddox asked gently.

"I can't be sure," said Mr. Blythe. "I must have fallen unconscious, for I awoke here in my home as an old man."

"Why haven't you tried to escape?" said Maddox.

"Look at me," Mr. Blythe said harshly. "I can't get out of this chair without help."

"But the brownies you have as staff, why couldn't they help you?"

Blythe took a moment to answer, as if he were having difficulty remembering. "My busyness has vanished and been replaced by another," he said finally. "They keep such a careful watch." He lowered his head, staring into his lap.

The front door to the house suddenly slammed shut. Mr. Blythe cast them a worried glance.

"I believe my attacker has finished up with his business outside," he said.

"I agree," said Maddox, "but who was the victor? Are you sure this new busyness isn't working for Thirsk?"

Mr. Blythe closed his eyes and said nothing.

"Right!" said Maddox. "Time to go: Chloe, help me get him up. Blythe can you walk? We're taking you with us."

"No!" cried Mr. Blythe. "I can't leave."

"Can't leave?" said Maddox.

"I need to stay," said Mr. Blythe, "I'm afraid I'll die if I leave my realm. It's hard to explain. I don't feel the connection to it the way I used to, but … I can't manage a journey, of this I'm certain."

"We can take you somewhere else," said Maddox. "You must have another residence?"

"Of course I do," coughed Mr. Blythe. "I have dozens of residences, but there's no time. Go! Find the mask. Bring it here so you can reverse what's been done. Please."

"I don't see a way out," said Chloe, looking at Maddox, "unless we can sneak out the back door like we planned. But your spell has stopped working."

"There's another way," said Mr. Blythe. "This is my house. Do you honestly believe I'd be unprepared given the state of things?"

"State of things?" said Maddox, raising an eyebrow.

"We don't have the time for an education," Mr. Blythe sighed. "You! Girl—open that cupboard. There's a passage in the floor. A simple spell conceals it. Just knock *Shave and a Haircut* to open it."

Heavy footsteps stomped up the stairs. Someone was coming.

"Quickly!" hissed Mr. Blythe, "Go now!"

Chloe and Maddox shuffled awkwardly into the small cupboard. Chloe knelt, knocking the familiar rhyme on the wooden floorboards. After the last knock, the faint outline of a concealed trap door appeared. An iron handle was set in its centre. She wrenched the trap door open. A blast of musty air wafted up. An iron ladder ran down into a gloomy crawlspace.

"No time to think about it," said Maddox. "Down you go!"

Chloe gripped the top of the ladder and plunged feet-first into the darkness. Maddox was soon behind her, pulling the hatch closed as he came. They descended several metres to a dusty floor. A few narrow beams of light spidered through the cracks above, barely illuminating the space.

Chloe and Maddox heard the door to the bedroom open. Someone rushed in. A volley of muffled voices followed—one aggressive, the other cowering. Maddox and Chloe only dared to move when they were sure Mr. Blythe's captor had gone.

"Ready to move?" said Maddox.

"Back up? Are you mad?" said Chloe. "You saw what

happened outside with the lightning and the fire?"

"Yes, I saw what happened," said Maddox distractedly, peering around them. "I wasn't suggesting a confrontation. We just need to be away from this place. You wouldn't happen to have any lint, would you?" he said.

Chloe reached into the pocket of her hoody. "Just this old sweets wrapper," she said, holding her hand out in the dim light.

"This will suffice," said Maddox, taking the wrapper. He made a few quick gestures, spinning the paper with his outstretched fingers. Holding it in his palm, he blew on it gently. The wrapper floated away, whirling excitedly like a flurry, rising up above their heads before bursting triumphantly into flames. The crawlspace was bathed in a warm light.

Chloe took a moment to take in her surroundings. They had climbed down into a space behind the wall on the north side of the house. It was a shelf of sorts with a rusted railing that ran on three sides, sparing them a fall from an unknowable height. The scuffed brick beneath her feet extended three paces to the left, becoming a staircase. The smell of damp stone was heavy in the air.

Maddox waved his hand, directing the spinning flame so it was in front of him.

"Careful of the *Ember*. It's hot," he said. "I've placed it in a thin shell so it can draw breath. But it's fragile and will burn anything that passes through its membrane. Come! Let's see where these stairs lead."

By the light of the *Ember*, Maddox stepped cautiously toward the stairs. Chloe followed.

"Do you think it's possible Blythe tricked us into coming down here?" she said.

"I thought of that," Maddox said over his shoulder, "but Blythe seems quite distressed over his situation. I doubt he'd be up to laying a trap for us."

"So you don't think it's strange there's a secret passageway leading away from the bedroom he's been trapped in?" said Chloe.

"It's very convenient," said Maddox mildly, "but most magicians have secret trapdoors and other ways of escape built into their homes."

"Do you?" said Chloe.

"I have a *Vidoy Door* in my flat which can whisk me away from any danger," said Maddox, "but that's it. Ixworth is always lecturing me about putting something similar in the workshop, but I've never gotten around to it."

"Not that I'm complaining," said Chloe, "but why?"

"I'm flattered you haven't noticed magicians are worry warts," said Maddox.

"But you know magic. What are you so frightened of?" said Chloe.

"Discovery," said Maddox. "We survive by keeping to ourselves. Not arousing suspicion. It's the only way one can linger in the same spot for countless years. Many of us learned this the hard way. Never underestimate the instructional power of a mob at your door accusing you of devilry, m'dear."

They stopped when they reached the bottom of the staircase. To the right, a tunnel of old brickwork ran away into darkness. The sound of dripping water rang distant. Maddox gestured, and the *Ember* led them away, twirling and casting odd patterns along the walls as it went.

"Why did Mr. Blythe say he might die if he left the house?" asked Chloe.

"I haven't a clue," said Maddox. "He seems to be suffering some type of detachment from his realm. I don't understand it."

"He looks like he's a hundred and fifty," said Chloe.

"He's younger than I am," said Maddox.

"I thought he was the same age as you?" said Chloe.

Maddox turned his head sharply. "You think I look as old and withered as Blythe?"

"Not now. Before. When he looked—youngish," said Chloe.

"Our situations are a little different," said Maddox. "He assumed his realm much later in life than I assumed mine. Oh! Look, Miss Chloe: I believe we've found our way out."

The *Ember* had stopped at the end of the passage beside a heavy iron door. They could see no discernible handle to unlock it. Maddox ran a hand across the cool metal. "It must be a simple spell to open it," he said. "One wouldn't want to be fussing about with anything too complicated if they were using this passage as an escape. The potent protection will be on the other side to stop anyone from entering."

"I'll take your word for it," said Chloe standing beside him. "It would be silly if we came all this way and got stuck by some stupid lock."

"Let's try the combination that unlocked the trapdoor," said Maddox. He knocked *Shave and a Haircut.*

The latch clunked and sighed, releasing its grip.

"You'll note, that was my first try," said Maddox, sounding pleased with himself. He gave the door a push, and it opened a crack. A draft of damp air blew inward. Leaning his weight against the door, he pushed again, and with a loud groan, it swung outward onto a lush, green park. A trimmed hedge grew to their right. Left, a birch fat with leaves. A pathway at its base led purposefully toward a nearby fountain. Water painted much of the grass and pavement in a hopscotch of puddles, a reminder of the day's earlier storm.

"As I suspected," said Maddox. "Holland Park."

Chloe turned back to inspect the door. It had been set in the wall beneath a drape of English ivy behind a bed of daffodils. "How long do you think this has been here?" she said.

"Probably something Blythe's father cooked up," said Maddox. "Let's return the door to its original state. It might prove useful at some other time, although I suspect finding and unlocking it again might be troublesome."

"Who do you think is holding Mr. Blythe captive?" said Chloe, remembering the exchange of magic outside Blythe's house.

Maddox was looking down distractedly at a tiny river of rainwater seeping from a nearby planter. "Your guess is as good as mine," he said. "A powerful magician. That I am certain."

"So, what now?" said Chloe, watching him.

Maddox sighed. "Home for us," he said. "I need some time to think about all this."

✦ ✦ ✦

"Did you see this?" said Dad, flipping around his paper. Much to Chloe's surprise it was a photo of Mr. Thirsk lying on his back on a rain soaked street. "This is from last night. Somebody took a picture with their mobile."

"I don't know what that is," lied Chloe. "Is it a man?"

Dad flipped his paper around to look at the photo again. "Of course it's a man. Says he was struck by lightning while out walking. It's been on the telly as well, on that breakfast show Mum likes to watch."

"Is he dead?" said Chloe, trying to sound disinterested.

"Says he was taken to the hospital," said Dad.

"That's all?" said Chloe.

"What else would you have it say?" Dad said.

Chloe shielded her face behind her mobile. "Nothing, I guess."

Dad shook his head sadly. "Honestly." He got to his feet, discarding his newspapers in a disorderly pile beneath his spot at the table, and wandered off toward the television.

Chloe waited until he had gone, then scurried on hands and knees to collect the paper. The photo of Mr. Thirsk was dark and grainy, but clearly he was worse for wear. His right arm appeared badly burnt and contorted at a strange angle. Chloe recalled the exchange: the magic on display was so different than anything she had seen Maddox or Ixworth conjure. Theirs seemed silly in comparison. Innocent. It was never meant to hurt anybody. Chloe shivered and then wrapped the paper into a roll. She would have to show this to Maddox.

✦ ✦ ✦

"We still don't have a lot to go on," said Maddox after Chloe arrived at the shop on Friday with the events of Mr. Blythe's house top of mind.

"But you're a magician," Chloe scolded. "Shouldn't you know something about this mask-thing Mr. Blythe mentioned?"

"I know a good many things about magical items," explained Maddox, "but this is something completely different."

"Because it turns people old," said Chloe.

"Precisely," said Maddox. He paused. "I wouldn't even know how to begin to create a spell that did that."

Chloe frowned. "I'm not trying to argue, but what's the difference between that and the hat racks? They bop people from one place to another. That seems pretty insane, no?"

"I agree," said Maddox. "But the hat racks are

probably based on a common spell—although somewhat modified. There are many ways to move from place to place. This mask, if it is actually a real thing, is something that requires a fundamental understanding of the ageing process, and that m'dear, is one of the great mysteries of life. There are just so many variables. It doesn't even seem possible."

"But somebody did it, unless Mr. Blythe is lying—or crazy," said Chloe.

"I don't know what to make of any of this," said Maddox sadly. "What we saw in Holland Park. Those spells that were being cast. It seems impossible."

"Perhaps Thirsk and the other magician have been studying," Chloe offered. "Doing research. I'm sure there's something on the internet."

Maddox shook his head. "Most of the information one would find by such means is utter nonsense. Remember what I said about magicians? We're solitary and secretive. We would never publish our work where it could be copied and read by others. It's too dangerous."

"Maybe one of them found it in a book," said Chloe. "Is there a magician's library somewhere?"

Maddox was silent, and sat staring at the ink drawings behind the counter. They seemed to occupy much of his free thoughts of late.

"Sorry," said Chloe, breaking the silence.

"Why are you sorry?" said Maddox.

"I feel like I'm being pushy."

Maddox waved a hand. "Nonsense. You're just trying to help. For that, I am grateful." He got up and stretched.

"We're going to figure this out," he said solemnly. "This mask—this thing that has taken away Blythe's youth—it seems to be part of the mystery, although we're no closer to discovering what happened to Ixworth nor the meaning of the strange note from his jacket." He paused for a moment, thinking. "There are no libraries of magic in London," he said, "at least none that I know. But there are other magicians. There's a chance one of them may know something."

Chloe noted his sullen expression. "You don't look happy."

Maddox smiled, trying to conceal the worry on his face. "I have someone in mind. This particular magician is one of the oldest in London. Perhaps the oldest."

"Have I heard of this person?" said Chloe.

"I may have referred to her but not by name. Miss Curzon. Her realm borders mine just south of here in Shepherd Market. It's a small realm. I don't go there."

"You don't go there or have never gone there?" said Chloe.

Maddox suddenly went pale.

"What's wrong with you?" said Chloe.

"This isn't going to be easy," said Maddox.

"Why?" said Chloe.

"Well, to tell you the truth," said Maddox, "Miss Curzon terrifies me."

CHAPTER 16

MISS CURZON

The sign on the shop front read:

Maddox's Extraordinary Curiosities.
Closed for Renovations.
Please visit us again in the fall.

It was written in a tidy, delicate script, an indication that the man who owned the business was intent on offering only the finest quality goods.

Chloe looked sadly at the sign. "Will you really open again in the fall?"

"I hope to," said Maddox, locking the shop door. "I've enjoyed my time as a shopkeep. In preparation, I've asked Mr. Winch to stay on. He has a wonderful eye. I feel he could craft some truly extraordinary pieces. But I need to close, at least for the time being. I just haven't been able to focus properly. Better to put the business aside for now and come back to it refreshed when all this is behind us."

Chloe turned to look at the gloomy shopfront window display. It was the first time she had seen it without any merchandise. "Will I still be allowed to drop by?" she said.

Maddox placed his shop keys in his pocket and turned toward Davis Street. "Miss Chloe. The shop wouldn't be the same without you."

They marched southward toward Shepherd Market. Where Fitzmaurice Place met Curzon Street, Maddox paused to quietly observe their surroundings.

"You never said why you're so scared of Miss Curzon," said Chloe.

Maddox kept his eyes on the street. "Magicians are competitive by nature. We do our best to hold onto our realms. Miss Curzon has a reputation for defending her borders. Vigorously. Even for minor incursions."

"What do you mean by minor incursions?" asked Chloe.

"More than two steps across her border," replied Maddox. "Most of us tolerate other magicians within our realms as long as they're passing through or conducting their affairs in an ordinary fashion."

"Like the ones who come to your shop to buy things?" said Chloe.

"Right," said Maddox. "It would be inconvenient to be bound to just one realm. Sometimes one needs to borrow a cup of sugar, if you know what I mean."

Chloe couldn't begin to imagine a lifetime confined to a single space, even one as large as Maddox's realm. "So, Miss Curzon doesn't like visitors."

"An understatement of epic proportions," said Maddox. "A colleague of mine from Crouch End once ventured into Shepherd Market for a haircut. He was *evicted* with such severity that he claims he can still feel his bones knocking whenever he draws close."

"Sounds like Miss Curzon has a bad temper," said Chloe.

"Why do you think I was so hesitant to come here?" said Maddox.

"Well, you're not getting a haircut," said Chloe. "Maybe I should just go. Where do I find her?"

Maddox considered Chloe's offer. "No. We need to do this together. Come, before I lose my nerve."

✦ ✦ ✦

They walked the north side of Curzon Street, crossing at the pedestrian crosswalk and then retracing their route on the opposite side of the street. Maddox looked nervous, his normal sophisticated swagger replaced by quick jerky movements. Turning south, they entered Shepherd Market tunnel. Maddox hurriedly ushered Chloe into a small breakfast nook. Inside, he chose a booth close to the door. Chloe waited while he ordered from the counter, and a moment later, he returned with tea. He set himself down beside Chloe on the bench facing the door.

"Did you tell someone at the counter we were here to see Miss Curzon?" said Chloe.

Maddox shook his head. "She's a bit of a hermit. I have no means of contacting her."

"How will we find her then?" said Chloe.

"She'll find us," said Maddox. "As soon as we left Fitzmaurice Place, she knew we were here. I'm hoping a public meeting will give us a chance to talk before an *Eviction*."

"That didn't help your Crouch End man," said Chloe, watching Maddox sip his tea nervously. "We're more than two steps within her borders."

Maddox put down his cup. "I'm hoping my charm and cleverness will extend a warm enough welcome. Oh! Goodness, that was quick. I believe we've been discovered."

Chloe looked up as a woman came in the door. She was dressed in black tights and a dark hoodie, the hood pulled snug over her head. Her boots were scuffed and marked, giving the impression they were used for unconventional purposes—like kicking or breaking things. Chloe had a strange feeling she had seen her before but wasn't sure where. In one smooth motion, the woman was at their booth, peering at them from beneath her hood with large green eyes.

"Why are you here?" she said sharply.

"Hullo-hullo," said Maddox. "We were hoping we could talk to Miss Curzon, if she's available."

The woman leaned over the table as if she were about to pounce. "Magicians aren't welcome here. You should know that. You need to leave. Now!"

"I understand Miss Curzon is not fond of people crossing her borders," said Maddox. "But I assure you, my visit is of great importance."

"I don't care," said the woman.

"You're not her, are you?" said Chloe defensively, feeling suddenly hot. She didn't like when people were mean to her friends.

The woman looked fiercely at Chloe. "What does it matter who I am?"

"We mean no harm," said Maddox. "My assistant Chloe and I are looking for some information. We believe Miss Curzon might be of some assistance."

The woman sat back, removing the hood. She was in her early twenties with dark cropped hair, sharp features, and a small diamond nose ring. She took something from her pocket and placed it on the table: a small, ornate snuff box with an engraved leaf on the lid. The woman popped the box open and pushed it in front of Maddox.

Maddox examined the box, then looked back at the woman, confused.

"And?"

"Say a few words," said the woman.

"I don't understand," said Maddox.

"Speak into it," the woman said impatiently.

Maddox lowered his head, and spoke awkwardly into the box, "Hullo-hullo?"

The woman rolled her eyes. "Your dad doesn't get out much, does he?" she said, looking at Chloe.

"Maddox, I think it's like a telephone. You talk into it," Chloe offered.

The woman nodded.

"Right-right-right," said Maddox, smiling sheepishly. "How silly of me." He leaned in close to the snuff box and cleared his throat. "Yes. We're hoping to speak with Miss Curzon about a matter, or matters of importance. My associate and I have discovered the existence of two powerful objects, an unreadable note and a mask, that have been made with especially strong magic. There are some extraordinary claims being made about the mask specifically. That is to say, that it can age a person. We also have a suspicion that it may give the wielder some right of ownership over another magician's realm. Although this is unconfirmed. Uh? That is all … thank you for your time. Goodnight. Rather, good morning."

The woman reached across the table and closed the lid of the snuff box. "This will only take a moment," she said.

There was an uncomfortable silence then. Chloe finished her tea and then wished she hadn't: would she be allowed to visit the lavatory?

The lid to the snuff box suddenly popped open all of its own. "Right," said the woman. "Come with me."

Miss Curzon lived directly above the Shepherd Market passage in a large flat which seemed to take up the entire third floor of the building. Getting to it had been confusing and befuddling. Chloe suspected this was deliberate. A safety measure. Like many of her experiences with magic, getting between here and there always seemed to take place in a manner out of time.

The woman in black led them from the breakfast nook to a door on the west side of Shepherd Market passage. Surprisingly, Chloe hadn't noticed it when they had passed the first time. It was handsome and red with a great iron knocker in the shape of a lion's head at its centre. The woman rapped once, waited a moment, then pushed open the door. They entered a narrow foyer. A staircase wound tightly to the third floor. They climbed to the top, turning sharply into a hallway and then stopped at another door, identical to the one below. The woman rapped the knocker three times, waited, then pushed it open as well. They proceeded down a hallway and turned sharply again. A third lion's head door barred their way.

"These doors will need different knocks when you leave," said the woman. "If you try to escape, you'll wander these halls forever."

"Are we prisoners, then?" said Maddox.

"That all depends on what business you have here," the woman replied, then knocked twice to let them in.

Chloe and Maddox stepped through and found themselves standing in a tiled entryway. A living area lay just beyond. At its heart, a lounger and love seat laden with blankets were positioned around a low coffee table stacked neatly with books. Four great windows, two on each side of the room, looked out over Curzon Street and Shepherd Market. Blossoming above, a tasteful chandelier bathed the space in a warm honey light. Chloe thought it one of the most lovely spaces she had ever set foot in.

The woman in black walked ahead, guiding them through a wide archway and then to the right into a large kitchen. A rough harvest table stood beneath a half-open window, where a pie sat cooling, filling the air with the glorious scent of cinnamon. On a rough shelf beside it, something wondrous swirled and bubbled in a large teacup on a saucer. An old spoon had been brought to life to whisk the odd mixture with clockwise circles, around and around, sugar and milk stirred into tea. There were knickknacks too: a surprised banana moon candle, three brightly coloured teapots in the shape of old homes, a delicate Russian doll, two carven chickadees, their heads turned to one another, gabbing. Chloe marvelled at everything: the furnishings, the old candy-floss-blue refrigerator, the tidiness. It seemed like such a safe and comfortable home.

They exited the kitchen through a paned door, stepping onto a wide rooftop terrace, enclosed by brick on three sides. The west side was open with a view of the market below. A privacy screen had been raised and grew wild with ivy. Flower pots in all shapes and sizes dotted the terrace. Some were alive with sunflowers, others with herbs. A group of plants farthest from the door were bursting with cherry tomatoes.

"Good heavens! That's Parsley Fern!" said Maddox, pointing to a group of odd plants in the corner of the secret garden, "And look! Anubis Pears. Marmalade Poppies! I didn't think there were any left."

"I'll ask you to keep your hands away from those," said a stern voice from behind them.

A woman dressed in enormous green wellington boots and a matching rain jacket stepped out from behind a group of ferns. She was tall, taller than Maddox, and moved with quick, surprisingly graceful movements for someone her age. For she was old. Very old. Despite this, the woman emitted a strange energy. Chloe couldn't help staring. The woman's eyes, behind thick glasses, were large and inquisitive, her mouth small, like a teardrop, jowls long, cheeks flushed pink, a head of grey hair cropped short.

"You should be glad I've let you see them," said the old woman. "It's rare for me to have visitors. Rarer still that they see my prized garden."

Maddox smiled warmly, clearing his throat, but the woman held up her hand flat before he could speak. "I don't want any nonsense from you, Mr. Maddox. I'm immune to your charms."

Maddox fumbled for words: "Thank you for seeing us, Miss Curzon. I know my company is probably unwelcome."

"Probably?" said Miss Curzon, pushing at her glasses. She nodded at the woman in black, who was still standing in the frame of the garden door. "Thank you, Mira. I can manage these two."

Mira closed the door and was gone.

"A helper?" inquired Maddox.

"Mira Butter?" said Miss Curzon. "Not a helper. Family."

Maddox gave Miss Curzon a puzzled look, but she seemed in no mood to explain.

"Who is this girl you've brought with you?" Miss Curzon asked, looking at Chloe.

"Chloe is a good friend of mine," said Maddox.

"Not a magician then?" said Miss Curzon.

"I'm afraid not," said Maddox. "But don't hold it against her."

"I think it does her credit," said Miss Curzon, looking Chloe up and down. "Not a magician, eh? How did you manage to get yourself mixed up with this one, Chloe?"

"A rather funny story ..." said Maddox.

"I wasn't speaking to you," Miss Curzon said sharply. She looked at Chloe again: "Never let a man speak for you. He'll end up saying something stupid, and that—ultimately—will reflect poorly on you."

"Sorry," said Chloe sheepishly. "We met by accident. I literally walked through the door to his shop and saw some of his brownies."

"Typical," tutted Miss Curzon, looking at Maddox. "No wonder you're in such trouble."

"Trouble?" said Maddox. "What kind of trouble am I in?"

Miss Curzon turned toward the door to the flat. "You better come inside," she said. "We'll need to get to the bottom of all this. I had planned on doing other things today, but you're here, so I guess that's that."

✦ ✦ ✦

"When I first came here, it was a blustery country market with more cattle than people," said Miss Curzon, standing by the window in her wellington boots.

They had returned to the large room with views of Curzon Street and Shepherd Market. Chloe and

Maddox had been invited to sit in the deep lounge chairs, yet Miss Curzon remained standing. Her large frame seemed even more enormous than it had outside.

Miss Curzon sighed, turning toward them. "Now, it's different. It feels different. I'm not sure I understand this new world, and I've never been one to shy away from progress."

"I believe I am of the same opinion," said Maddox. "It's one of the reason's we—I—decided to open a legitimate business. I felt it best to keep an open mind. One foot in the new world, one in the old."

"I don't think you and I are talking about the same thing," said Miss Curzon.

"Oh?" said Maddox.

"I wasn't referring to that silly modern world," said Miss Curzon, nodding toward the window. "No offence to you, Chloe. After all, it is yours."

"That's okay," said Chloe. "It sometimes feels weird to me too."

"Progress has always seemed miraculous, especially when one isn't limited to a normal life span," continued Miss Curzon. "Electricity, running water, the lavatory—magic. But what I'm talking about is the magician's world."

"I'm not sure I understand," said Maddox. "How is life changing for us?"

Miss Curzon rolled her eyes. "You wouldn't be here if things were normal, would you?"

Maddox thought for a moment. "I suppose not," he said finally. "Things have changed for me, but I don't believe my problems have anything to do with the rest of London's magicians."

"Don't they?" said Miss Curzon.

"Is there something you're not telling me?" said Maddox, frowning. "You're being a bit vague."

"And you're being dramatic," said Miss Curzon, waving a hand. "It doesn't suit you." She looked at Chloe: "Tell me why he's brought you here."

Chloe swallowed, fearful of upsetting their host. "We're wondering if you know anything about a magical mask."

"I might," said Miss Curzon. "Go on—have you seen it?"

"No," said Chloe, "another magician told us about it."

"Perhaps it's just a rumour then," said Miss Curzon.

"Maybe," said Chloe.

"Seems an elaborate story to be just a rumour, wouldn't you say?" said Maddox.

Miss Curzon shot him a stern look but turned back to Chloe. "Your associate says the mask ages a person. Have you actually seen this effect, or is this also a rumour?"

"We saw," said Chloe.

"Yes? And who?"

"Mr. Blythe," answered Chloe. "I wanted to feel sorry for him, but at the time—now, even—I'm not so sure I do. I suppose I'm a little sorry. I guess it's rude not to feel bad when something rotten happens to somebody."

For the briefest of moments, Miss Curzon's mouth curled into a smile. "I'm sure he had it coming," she said.

"So, he's aged? How much? And tread carefully if you're going to be making any comparisons to me."

"Old," said Chloe. "Old enough he's stuck in a chair."

Miss Curzon's eyes fell to the window that overlooked the market. It was a moment before she spoke again. "Magical objects are as common as the clouds outside this window, yet …" She turned to face them. "The *Tyburn Mask* matches your description to a degree. But its existence is questionable, and its history, much like your story, is based on rumour."

"I know of Tyburn," said Maddox. "I can recall stories from when I was a boy. About a magician so scarred, he was forced to cover his face. 'Stick to your curfews. Beware the Pasture Lands Devil,' they would say. But I imagined his mask being more like the one worn by Guy Fawkes. A symbol."

"There is a kernel of truth in most stories," said Miss Curzon.

Chloe cleared her throat: "May I ask: who is Tyburn?"

Maddox gave Miss Curzon an opportunity to answer, then spoke: "He was a magician from early London, but I don't know very much about him."

"I know some," added Miss Curzon. "A few stories, but not much more. I never met him. A relief considering he owned much of Mayfair and his realm bordered mine."

"Mayfair wasn't always yours?" said Chloe, looking at Maddox.

"London is nearly two thousand years old," said

Maddox, shaking his head. "I'm a single page in its huge history."

Miss Curzon left the window and eased herself onto the love seat beside them. "Tyburn's name is taken from the River Tyburn, the realm he chose in those early years. A wise decision at the time, for it gave him control of a large section of the city. South Hampstead, Mayfair, Westminster, Pimlico, maybe even as far as Vauxhall. But his greed was his undoing. Like most of our realms, his suffered the demands of an expanding city. As industry and prosperity grew, the river began to fade. People drew from it, used it as a resource. It became a fraction of what it was. Tyburn grew weak. His life and power, tied so closely to the river's waters, began to slip away. In desperation, he tried to acquire the realms of others. Scheming and swindling at first, but when that didn't succeed, he resorted to other means. Kidnapping. Murdering. Stealing. Anything to save his life. Some said he wore a special mask when he came upon his prey. A mask that could steal their magic, masterfully crafted using a spell a hundred years in the making. Others suggested the mask was used to conceal his identity as he carried out his crimes. Others believed it was forged by Old Magic and had some other purpose."

"Did he ever try to take your realm?" said Maddox.

"Tyburn focussed his energies in the north where the magicians were young and less experienced, but it was frightening for all of us. About then, some of London's magicians got together to discuss what was to be done. That was the beginnings of the Magicians'

Guild. They agreed to take action. I never did learn the exact details of Tyburn's banishment or death, for it was a quiet and hushed affair. Afterward, an agreement was put together regarding the granting of realms and the process of inheritance. As you know, one can't simply claim a realm as one's own. There is a natural process to magic. It never passes immediately from one to another."

Miss Curzon grew silent and looked again to the window.

"If this is the real *Tyburn Mask*, what is its purpose?" said Maddox. "Did he dispatch his victims by ageing them? I can think of better ways to be rid of someone. Besides, his magic was dwindling, how could he fashion such a thing using Old Magic? Are any of us strong enough to do that even when healthy?"

Miss Curzon shrugged stiffly, showing her age for the first time. "This is where fact and rumour become more jumbled," she said. "It is assumed Tyburn had help from Abandinus."

Chloe looked at Maddox for an explanation, but he said, "That word is unfamiliar to me."

"It's a very old name," said Miss Curzon, "one with little meaning to most. Abandinus was a Primeval. A god, or godlike to some, although one of local designation. More than likely he was a magician or warlock like you and me, but very powerful. Legend has it Abandinus was driven from his realm in Cambridgeshire and ended up here in London. The rest, like his relationship with Tyburn, the mask's origin—symbol or not—and how it was forged, remains a mystery."

Maddox sat massaging his temples, trying to soothe this new information into his head.

"I'm at a loss," he said finally. "There are too many odds and ends to this mystery. There seems to be no reasonable explanation for anything."

"You still haven't told me what this great mystery is," said Miss Curzon.

"There's nothing to tell. I don't know anything," said Maddox. "Mr. Blythe asked for our help."

Miss Curzon sighed. "That's a lie," she said curtly. "Why would you go out of your way to help that man?" Her eyes narrowed. "You mentioned going into business. Where is Mr. Ixworth, as a matter of interest? You've made no mention of him."

Maddox shifted his weight uncomfortably.

Miss Curzon turned to address Chloe. "Are you aware I knew Mr. Maddox when he was a young man?"

Chloe shook her head.

"Actually, he wasn't a man," said Miss Curzon. "A boy. Not much older than you. I caught him pinching cabbages in my market. He would use his tricks to fool the local vendors. I taught him a lesson, punishment for using magic to benefit himself at the expense of others. Too bad I couldn't have done the same to his wicked master. He probably put him up to it. I hoped Maddox had changed his ways. Alas, I still see he's up to his old deceptions."

Maddox stared at his shoes.

"So, Maddox, are you going to tell me the rest?" said

Miss Curzon. "Or are you going to waste more of my time and yours."

"I apologise," said Maddox tiredly. "Please understand, my goal is not deception. I only wish to protect my friend. Ixworth has been missing for weeks, and the more we investigate, the more muddled things have become."

Miss Curzon sat watching Maddox,waiting for him to speak again.

"I found this in his jacket pocket," said Maddox, removing Ixworth's tattered copy of the *Quarterly Crow*. He handed it to Miss Curzon. "I was—am still—unable to read it, yet Chloe, remarkably, was able to shed some light on what it contains. I have no idea what it is."

Miss Curzon carefully unfolded the bulletin. She read for only a second before the strain became evident on her face as it had been for Maddox. She looked up briefly, scanning Chloe and Maddox, and for a moment Chloe was worried Miss Curzon thought they were trying to trick her. But then the elderly woman closed her eyes, and after taking three deep breaths, continued to read. When she finished reading both sides of the bulletin, she gave it back to Maddox and sat for a long moment with her eyes closed.

"That thing you have in your possession, Maddox," she said finally, "is a *Greave Note*."

"I'm at a loss," said Maddox. "I don't know what that is."

"Nor should you," said Miss Curzon. "This is dark material—Old Magic. Very strong and difficult to create. It probably took years. Decades even. There isn't a magician in London who could conjure one by themself. Which is worrisome, for it must have been cast by more than one, and if two, three, perhaps even more magicians were stupid enough to try to make one together, it would make the spell especially unstable and near impossible to control."

"But what is its purpose?" said Maddox. "Why did Ixworth have it?"

"Like the name suggests, the spell uses grief to trigger a reaction in the reader of the note. The victim."

"But I was unable to read it," said Maddox, "and Chloe doesn't seem to have suffered any effects."

"Yes, lucky that," said Miss Curzon, with a clear note of disappointment. "You should never have let her touch it, let alone read it."

Maddox looked at his shoes again. "I still don't understand."

Miss Curzon sighed. "Somewhere, hidden in or between the words of the *Greave Note*, lies a terrible truth. The sentences may seem nonsensical to you and I, but we are not the intended victim."

"Ixworth!" cried Maddox, a look of horror on his face.

"Maybe," said Miss Curzon. "Actually—very likely."

"But how? Why?" said Maddox dumbly.

Miss Curzon gave Maddox a cold stare. "It seems obvious to me," she said fiercely. "The mask and the *Greave Note* are connected. Each has a purpose, one for the other."

"That doesn't help me much," said Maddox bitterly.

Miss Curzon looked at Maddox dismissively "It's no coincidence you and Tyburn are connected, Maddox. The Mask is bound to your realm. Haven't you been listening? Perhaps that is the missing piece to your puzzle?"

Miss Curzon climbed to her feet.

"You mind yourself," she said, addressing Chloe. "These magicians are not to be trusted. Even the nice ones." She gave Maddox a final disapproving look. "Mira will show you the way out now."

She turned away then, her tall frame stooping slightly. Halfway to the kitchen she stopped, speaking over her shoulder: "You've brought two disturbing things to my attention today, Maddox. It's too late to stop the *Greave Note*. I think that card has already been played, and nothing can be done to stop it. But it sounds like the *Tyburn Mask* is still in play, and if it is real and your story isn't some silly nonsense used to cover up one of your schemes, then its purpose is evil, and nothing good will come of its use."

CHAPTER 17

BEHIND THE WALL

Chloe recalled one of her teachers once saying it was important to know how one felt. It was a part of a lecture on self esteem. At the time, it had seemed a silly thing to say. She always knew how she felt. Wasn't it obvious? Anyone who didn't must be mad. Yet, on her walk to the shop the day after meeting Miss Curzon, Chloe was unsure how she felt about a lot of things: about magic, about becoming a magician. It had all seemed so fun when she'd first started coming around the curiosity shop. But recent events made her realise things had become serious. Deadly serious. Turning onto South Molten Lane, Chloe noted a smartly dressed man standing outside the shop. As she approached, he turned and smiled. Chloe recognized the deep crinkly lines of his face immediately. Mr. Pudding: the Alderman's chauffeur.

"Nice to see you again," he said with a nod. For a moment Chloe wasn't sure what to do. If Mr. Pudding was here, surely Mr. Hustings was too. Maddox was probably busy. She turned with a mind to head back home.

"You can go inside," said Mr. Pudding, motioning

toward the door. "I think Mr. Hustings and Mr. Maddox are probably close to finishing up their business." He looked at his watch. "They've been chatting a while."

Chloe's heart sank. Was Maddox in trouble? This was her fault. If only she had been able to keep her mouth shut. Taking a nervous breath, she entered the shop, leaving Mr. Pudding waiting outside.

Maddox was seated behind the counter with his arms folded. The man standing in front of the register must have been Hustings, but in a way, Chloe felt like she was seeing him for the first time, for he was no longer dressed in shadows. Yet his aura of sophistication remained. A boss. As Chloe entered, his cat-like eyes pounced, watching her every move.

"Good afternoon, Miss Ashley," he said, his sharp features working themselves into a smile. "Up and about, I see. Have you recovered from your unfortunate episode?"

Chloe stopped a few feet from the register. "Yes, I'm all better now," she said, swallowing.

Mr. Husting's smile grew wider. "No need to fret," he said gently. "You can approach. We're all friends here."

Maddox gave Chloe a nod, and she came around the counter. Once she was settled, Mr. Hustings spoke again.

"Maddox and I were just discussing hat racks," he said mildly. "Of all the subjects in the world two gentlemen could discuss, can you imagine that? Hat racks."

Chloe wasn't sure if she was supposed to answer. Luckily Maddox interjected, "It is a strange and bizarre world we live in, wouldn't you say, Hustings?" He folded his hands neatly in front of him. "I once knew a man from Wall End who bewitched an old washtub with a *Dorathy-Diggs*. He refused to walk. Take a carriage. Anything. It was the only acceptable way for him to get from place to place. Oi, the things we would say behind his back."

"Wall End?" said Mr. Hustings holding his chin. "Mr. Caulfield, wasn't it? Yes, I remember him. He did have an odd temperament. And a habit of complaining. I can recall nine letters received by my office in a single year. Never a dull moment." Mr. Hustings turned to Chloe. "Apologies, Miss Ashley," he said, winking. "I'm sure you don't want to listen to two old magicians relive the past, do you?"

Chloe tried to smile, but ended up shrugging instead. "Maddox does tell a lot of stories," she said. And then regretted saying it. She didn't want Mr. Hustings to think she was making fun of Maddox.

Mr. Hustings smiled and turned back to Maddox. "You'll let me know if you uncover anything, yes?"

Maddox nodded. "Yes, of course," he said and then folded his arms again.

Mr. Hustings nodded. Turning, he walked toward the door. "One thing worth mentioning," he said over his shoulder. "I dropped by Ixworth's residence. Miss Ashley mentioned she hadn't seen him in a few days. Where did you say he was, Maddox?"

"Just out of town for a few days on business," Maddox replied.

"Oh, that's right," said Mr. Hustings, nodding. "His house does appear to be in good order. But the odd thing is I didn't really get a good sense of him. The house had such an un-Ixworth-like essence about it, if that makes any sense?" Mr. Hustings paused, looking at them intently. "Any chance you know how long he'll be away?"

Maddox shrugged. "I expect him back any day now."

Mr. Hustings nodded, and for a moment, it appeared he was about to say something else. Instead, he smiled and left, closing the shop door quietly behind him.

It was a long moment before either Chloe or Maddox spoke.

"I'm so sorry, Maddox," said Chloe, finally breaking the silence.

"You have no reason to be sorry," said Maddox.

"But I'm the reason Mr. Hustings is snooping around."

Maddox smiled kindly. "No, you just happened to get caught up in Hustings's snoopings, as you call them. The Alderman is looking into Blythe's disappearance."

"But he was asking about the hat racks," said Chloe. "What did you tell him?"

"I told him the truth," said Maddox. "The appearance of the hat racks is rather mysterious. One in my workshop. One at Blythe's. In the park. Three at the house you visited. Hustings thought it odd too. I also mentioned Mr. Thirsk has been sneaking about."

Chloe's eyes grew wide. "Does Hustings think Thirsk is the one who kidnapped Blythe?"

"The Alderman is a difficult man to read," said Maddox, removing a slip of paper and a pen from one of the drawers beneath the counter. "Besides, Thirsk can't be the one who kidnapped Blythe. He was attacked by that person in the hood outside Blythe's house."

Chloe recalled the strange hooded figure and their crazy use of magic. Mr. Thirsk had suffered greatly. "But you lied about Ixworth," said Chloe.

Maddox looked thoughtful. "Not so much a lie," he said. "More wishful thinking. I'm hoping we can unravel this mystery and find Ixworth before Hustings needs to get involved." Maddox tapped a finger on the paper in front of him. "Ready to do some detective work? I've jotted down some notes. It's all the bits and bobs we know so far."

Chloe examined the paper closely. Maddox had written "Ixworth" in the middle of the page and then a number of words and short sentences in circles around his name: hat racks; empty shop; three missing magicians (one found!); *Tyburn's Mask*; *Greave Note*; Thirsk sneaking around; unknown magician (wearing a hood!); wild magic.

"Am I missing anything?" said Maddox.

Chloe read, and re-read the paper several times.

"The pushpin map," said Chloe.

"Of course!" said Maddox, taking the paper and jotting it down in the top left beside *Greave Note*.

"What about the brownies I overheard? They said they were going to make spells to protect that house I landed in. Because someone was sneaking around."

"Right-right," said Maddox. "They were probably talking about Thirsk, but I suppose we can add that." He paused his pen. "Hold on a moment."

"What is it?" said Chloe.

"The brownies were taking precautions at the house. Casting spells and whatnot. But why add another spell to the hat rack? They were the ones using it."

Chloe scratched at her nose. "They said the hat rack was undetectable, but they were going to send someone to add something to make it extra safe."

"But they were making those plans before they knew we had found it and before you had used it," said Maddox. "And there's no way they could have added any extra protection. I cast an *Ebenezer's Mirror*. Remember? The hat rack is unusable. At least from their side. I suppose there's a chance they never got around to it, but—are you sure they said they were adding protection to the hat rack?"

"They said workshop entrance, I think," said Chloe.

Maddox scratched at his beard. "Yes, I think you and I just assumed it was the hat rack. But maybe that's not what they were talking about."

"You don't think ...?—Didn't you say Ixworth was always nagging you about making a secret entrance?" said Chloe.

"I did say that," said Maddox.

"Maybe he created one without you knowing about it," said Chloe. "And then someone came around the hat rack and that's how he escaped!"

"Yes-yes-yes, very true," said Maddox. He moved

out in front of the counter and began pacing. "Let's stay with this thought for a moment," he said, wagging his finger. "If there's another way to get in and out of the workshop, then somebody besides Ixworth might have known about it. Why else would they be trying to protect it?"

"It seems weird to protect the entrance to an empty workshop," said Chloe, matter-of-factly. "Unless there's something else in your shop they want."

"Or ..." said Maddox, stopping in his tracks. "The entrance itself is what they're after. Perhaps it's not coming into the shop, but leading away from it."

"That could have been the way all the stuff was taken out of the workshop in a single night," said Chloe excitedly. "We need to find it! It could lead us to Ixworth."

Maddox was already moving toward the door to the storeroom. "It may end up leading us to a whole lot more," he said.

✦ ✦ ✦

"There's no need to worry about that old hat rack," said Maddox, noting the wary look Chloe gave it as they entered the basement workshop. "Remember? The *Ebenezer's Mirror*? It's been cast around it. A person coming around is going to bounce right back again."

Chloe nodded but stood well clear anyway. "You said something about the secret entrance leading away from the workshop. Why would somebody want that?"

"I was thinking about that in the lift," said Maddox,

examining the weathered brick of the workshop wall to the left of the entrance. "Remember the pushpin map? It tells us someone has been looking for something, evident by the marked locations. Locations mind you, in Mayfair. Why Mayfair, why those exact locations?"

Chloe thought for a brief moment. "They were looking for *Tyburn's Mask*!"

"Exactly," said Maddox. "Tyburn's river realm is diminished, but it isn't lost altogether. It still exists, it's just buried beneath the city. And the course of the old river runs right through my realm, steps from this very spot. Miss Curzon said the *Tyburn Mask* is bound to this realm. You see? I think this second entrance might be the way somebody has been searching for it."

"But we don't even know if there is a second entrance," said Chloe. "And if there is, then who made it? It couldn't have been Ixworth: he's the one who's missing."

Maddox was pacing feverishly. "True. Unless it's both? An escape from the workshop and a way to access the rest of my realm. We just don't know."

Chloe felt a sudden pang of emotion for Maddox, confused and sad, his best friend gone. She took four large steps into the abandoned workshop and turned to face him.

"Right," she said, "how do we find it?"

Maddox stopped his pacing and came to stand beside Chloe. "That's a very good question. Normally I would just make a sweep of the room. I would get a sense of any unusual magic that was being used to conceal an entranceway."

"Sorry to sound mean," said Chloe looking at him, "but you didn't pick up on the hat rack. And that was sitting right out in the open where you could see it."

"Very true," said Maddox. "And the Billyfish would have sniffed out anything I missed." He sighed heavily, leaning his back against the wall.

Chloe tried to remember all the details of Blythe's secret door in his guest room. It seemed ridiculously obvious once it had been revealed to them. "What if the entrance is real?" said Chloe.

"What do you mean, real?" said Maddox.

"The passage—the door—whatever it is. What if it's not magic?"

Maddox stepped away from the wall. "Then neither I nor the Billyfish would have been able to discover it." He began pacing again. "It makes perfect sense: why spend all your energy casting a powerful spell when you can just hide something practically? Miss Chloe, you are a genius!"

Maddox began to walk slowly, taking small well-placed steps while raking his outstretched fingers along the wall of the workshop. Chloe searched too, inspecting the wall nearest her. Together they combed the workshop, taking their time to examine each brick they passed. After ten minutes, they had covered half of the empty space. Chloe took a break, sitting crossed-legged on the floor opposite Maddox.

Maddox sighed, turning his back to the wall. "Perhaps I got a little too excited," he said solemnly. "This seems like a fruitless search."

From her seated position, Chloe noticed something,

just to the right of Maddox's shoe. A discoloured brick, a shade different than the rest.

"What's that?" she said.

"You've found something?" said Maddox.

"Just there, near the floor," she said, pointing. "You see it?"

Maddox crouched, poking the brick with his finger. It moved. Gripping the edges, he managed to pull it free.

"What is it?" said Chloe, kneeling beside him.

"It's too dark to see," said Maddox, "I'd investigate further, but I'm wary of reaching my hand into a trap." He stood suddenly, scanning the floor, then walked a few paces to retrieve a pinch of sawdust, a remnant of the bustling workshop from weeks before. He spun an *Ember* with a few quick motions and then, with a wave, lowered the playful flame to the floor, where it cast its pale light on the hole. He crouched again, looking in.

"You've become quite skilled at solving riddles, Miss Chloe," said Maddox.

"You see something?"

Maddox reached his hand into the opening. "A lever," he said, giving it a stiff tug. Something suddenly whirred to life: gears popped and wound, then there came a sound like shifting metal. A section of the wall opened inward, revealing a darkened passage.

"I'm dreaming this," said Chloe. "I've seen some insane things, but this is too much."

"I agree," said Maddox. "It's beyond belief."

"How long has this been here without you knowing about it?" said Chloe.

"Hard to say," said Maddox, casting the light of the *Ember* through the doorway. "Someone has been very careful and very meticulous in the making of this passage. But it could have been made at any time, perhaps even before Ixworth and I started our business."

A musty smell with a copper tang wafted up out of the passage.

"What is that?" said Chloe. "I've smelled it before. From the top of the lift."

"That is the sweet perfume of buried water," said Maddox. "I've been attributing that odour to the belch of old basements, or more rudely, a byproduct of a busy brownie workshop."

They stood for another moment staring into the darkened passage.

"Miss Curzon said the River Tyburn flowed near here," said Chloe. "A river below a city seems a magical thing. Are we going?"

"Not yet," said Maddox. "Who knows where this leads? I'll need time to prepare. As you've reported, those brownies you overheard said they were going to send someone to cast extra measures. Most likely those are traps. It's bound to be dangerous."

CHAPTER 18

BENEATH THE CITY

Chloe stood for a long moment peering into her closet. She was feeling conflicted. What exactly was one supposed to wear when descending into the belly of London? Ordinary trousers? Jeans? Tights? Boots for sure. A sweater. Definitely a tuque. Chloe half wondered if she should be equipping herself with spells. Maddox had said venturing through the secret passageway was bound to be dangerous. But what were these dangers? Surely not a dragon. Or something living. For a moment Chloe struggled to remember the purpose of their explorations. Was it to find the *Tyburn Mask*? Search for the mysterious hooded magician who had put Mr. Thirsk in the hospital and used the mask on Mr. Blythe? At first, she suspected it should have been all of these reasons. But for her, the only real goal was finding her friend Ixworth.

Maddox greeted Chloe at the door to the shop. He was dressed in his usual attire: neat pants, jacket and bow tie. His mood was drab. Chloe might have pressed him—asked how he was doing, but she didn't feel like talking. The seriousness of their errand weighed on her mind. Probably Maddox's too. Chloe followed him to the lift, and they descended to the basement in silence, each alone with their thoughts. As they came into the workshop, some of Chloe's worry evaporated and was replaced with excitement. They were a step closer to finding out what had happened to Ixworth. She thought of all the lovely things about him. The books, the chats, their indoor picnics. She hoped he was okay.

"There's sawdust on the floor here," said Chloe, standing in front of the entrance to the darkened passageway in the wall of the workshop. "For an *Ember*."

Maddox stood beside her. "That won't be necessary," he said, pulling a slender black torch from his jacket pocket. "The practical nature of this hidden door got me thinking. I have no idea what traps have been set. The last thing we need is an *Inoculation* knocking out an *Ember* and us fumbling about in the dark."

Chloe wondered where Maddox had bought the torch and whether it had been a hurried alternative to preparing a spell of some kind.

"I'm not keen on rats," she said, keeping her hands close to her sides.

"Nor I," said Maddox, switching on the torch. A cone of light illuminated a small stretch of corridor, grey-bricked and dreary. "Let's hope there are none. Stay behind me. If there are traps, it would be best if they were sprung by me."

They entered the passage cautiously, footfalls

echoing hollow, the sense of water tickling their noses. Around them, the city thrummed, sound coursing through the stone like a pulse, punctuated by the rumble of a lorry or the knock of a car crossing a manhole cover. They walked for a while and then descended a shallow staircase. A door stood at the bottom, as black as an old steam engine. Its shell seemed to absorb sound. Chloe touched the cold iron with her palm.

"I hope you've brought something strong to open this," she said.

"I think I have just the thing," said Maddox, nudging Chloe gently aside. He pulled a small bottle from his pocket and removed the stopper. It contained a fine powder. Carefully, he poured the contents out, forming the shape of a square directly in front of the door.

"What's that supposed to do?" said Chloe.

"It's an *Og Saw*," said Maddox. "It's old. Invented by Kashka à la Lune, the greatest thief of all time. Later picked up by pickpockets and thieves when I was a younger magician. It removes safeguards. Here, watch."

Chloe looked on: the space within the powdered square began to change, slowly at first, and then quickly, like water drying on hot pavement. The shape of a blackened door began to appear atop the brick of the passage floor. At the same time, the door blocking their path began to fade, becoming a transparent ghostly thing, and then nothing at all.

"Wait-wait-wait," cried Chloe. "What just happened?"

"Door to floor," said Maddox triumphantly. "No disassembly. No cracking or breaking. The *Og Saw* takes an obstacle and moves it somewhere else. Out of your way. It's very useful for those stealing artwork. Casually sprinkle some of this in front of a painting, and in just a few seconds, one has it. No mess. No fuss."

Chloe placed a foot on the door near her feet to test that it was real. "Can I have some of that potion, please?"

Maddox frowned, shining the torch into the passage beyond the door. "I can just imagine what an eleven-year-old would get up to with a vial of this," he said. "The only way you're getting any is if you make it yourself."

They passed through the doorway, entering another passage, much wider than the first. Along the walls, close to the floor, the stonework was stained dark with mould. At the passage's centre, the floor slanted downward to a channel of oily water.

"Is that a sewer?" said Chloe.

Maddox had stopped, paying careful attention to what lay before them. "Not a sewer. The River Tyburn."

"Like the real River Tyburn? " said Chloe. "Like Miss Curzon told us? The one that Tyburn took as his realm?"

"The very one," said Maddox.

"It seems so weird," said Chloe. "This is your realm."

"Remember, it hasn't always been mine," said Maddox. "London is a very old city. Many magicians have held realms here well before my time. There's a lot of history buried in this soil."

"Doesn't seem much of a river," said Chloe, noting the lazy flow of the water below them. "Which way do we go?"

"Luckily there's only one way we can go," said Maddox, motioning to the left where the channel emptied into a narrower tunnel that sloped downward in the direction of the Thames. "A relief. I was worried how much ground we would need to cover. These catacombs are endless. A poor decision could send us off into the dark on some misguided adventure. But our decision has been made for us. We can assume we're on the right track."

Chloe sighed. "I'm not sure what I expected, but it seems weird we would find Ixworth here," she said. "I guess we can say we were right—there was a secret passage into the workshop. But what does it all mean?"

Maddox nodded. "I wish I could be sure," he said. "The *Tyburn Mask* is a big part of this mystery. Somebody has gone through great pains to find it. And it would seem—at least according to Blythe—it was used on him. I don't think it's a coincidence the River Tyburn is within my realm and just steps from my workshop. I'm hoping something here will give us a clue to Ixworth's whereabouts."

"At least we know somebody else has come this way," said Chloe, noting several muddy footprints on the brick just within reach of the torchlight. They led away to the right before disappearing into the dark.

"Yes," said Maddox, his face grim in the dim light. "Let's follow and see where they lead."

They headed away from the outflow, following a narrow shelf alongside the channel. There was a similar space on the opposite side, but the brickwork was crumbling, and the stone was slick with algae. The likelihood of a fall was high. Following the channel northward, they found little: a fallen brick, a plastic bag in the shape of a cape, old tins and bottles, items discarded or washed away and forgotten. As they walked, the passage narrowed, bringing them close to the sluggish river water. For the last leg of their journey, they scurried like crabs across a slippery table of stone and finally dropped down the other side into another section of the passage. Ahead, the channel spread greedily across the entire width of the space. To go further would mean a dip in dark water.

"There's magic at work here," said Maddox, casting the torch light on the walls of the chamber for a sign of the unordinary.

"This is a perfect place for a trap," said Chloe, eying the pool that ran away from their feet into darkness.

"Perhaps," said Maddox, "although, everything we've seen so far was put in place to conceal. Perhaps a trap would bring too much attention."

"That makes a lot of sense," said Chloe. "Especially if the trap got sprung and the person got away. They'd wonder what it was protecting. You said you sensed magic at work?"

"Yes. Fluttering and flustering. A definite nagging from somewhere in that direction." He pointed.

Chloe gave him a funny look.

"Sorry, I'm not being very clear, am I?" said Maddox. "The sensation is difficult to explain properly. But imagine if this were a room in your house, like your bedroom. You know where you put your things. The order of your photographs. The placement of a favourite book. The way you make your bed. You would recognize something if it were out of place, yes?"

"Of course," said Chloe. "Dad comes into my room all the time to steal my mobile charger."

"Exactly!" said Maddox. "Somebody's stolen my mobile charger."

"I don't think that's what you mean," said Chloe.

Maddox shrugged. "What I'm trying to say is there's magic across the way over there, and it sticks out like a sore thumb." He turned, shining the torch on a low step that had been bricked into the base of the wall on the other side of the passage. It didn't seem to have a purpose. "Think you can jump that far?" he said.

Chloe motioned toward Maddox's loafers. "I think you should be more worried about you jumping over that mess. I wore trainers."

"I'll go first then," said Maddox. "You and your trainers can pull me out if I'm unsuccessful."

Chloe was tempted to take a picture with her mobile. She would call it *Maddox Taking a Bath in the River Tyburn*. They would laugh about it later, but the seriousness of their situation stopped her, and she decided instead to just watch things unfold.

After giving his jacket a pat to ensure the contents of his pockets were secure, Maddox stepped toward the channel. Then, with one hand gripping the torch, he took a giant leap across the water.

"I'm younger than I look," he said, beaming back from the far side of the passage. "Now you."

Chloe edged forward, trying her best to ignore the consequences of a failed attempt. She tested the stone to ensure she had traction, then leapt across.

"Well done, Miss Chloe," said Maddox. "Now, have a look at this." He directed her attention to a small nook cut into the wall in front of the step, large enough for a person to stand in. He reached his arm into the space and ran his hand along the back of the wall. "The spells are focused here."

"More than one?" said Chloe. "Is that going to be a problem?"

"I think I can manage it," said Maddox. "But it's a strange combination of magic. New and old. The new was cast on top of what was here before."

"Just be careful," said Chloe. "My *Rosebud* won't be able to help you if something goes wrong.

"I have no desire to be burned to ashes," Maddox joked, stepping into the enclosure. He closed his eyes, trying to get a sense of the magic. "I think it's a door charm," he began, "extremely strong, but I think I ..." A funny look came over his face.

"Are you all right?" said Chloe.

Maddox stared back at her.

"What's wrong with you? Have you unlocked the door?" said Chloe.

Maddox's face was pale and had the panicked

expression of someone who had just witnessed something terrible. Chloe grabbed him by the front of his coat, pulling him away from the wall. His full weight collapsed forward, knocking her over, and she felt the hot bite of the stone floor scrape at her arms. The torch bounced away and went out. The passage was plunged into darkness.

Chloe felt icy fingers of panic creep up her back.

"Maddox!" she hissed. "Maddox!" Her voice echoed oddly, a boomerang of sound going away and then returning at a lower pitch. She reached out with her hand, searching for the torch but the cool waters of the Tyburn were all she discovered. Her mobile seemed a good temporary option. It woke as she pulled it from her pocket, casting a pale light around them. Maddox was near, lying on his back with his eyes open.

"Are you alive?" she said, gently shaking him. "Wake up!"

Maddox moved, muttering.

"Maddox!" cried Chloe. "The torch has gone out. We're in the dark. Say something so I know you're okay."

"I've never really been a big fan of parsley," he said shakily.

"That's not what I meant," Chloe cried. "What happened to you?"

"I was hoping you could tell me," said Maddox.

"You weren't talking."

"How long was I like that?" said Maddox, sitting up and wiping his brow with the back of his hand.

"A few seconds. Maybe more," said Chloe.

"Just that?" he said. "It felt longer. Seemed like always, if that means anything."

"You have to be more careful," Chloe said crossly. "You said there would be traps, and you've just fallen headfirst into the first one we've come across."

"Indeed I have," said Maddox, smiling weakly. "Forgive me."

"So you don't know what happened?" said Chloe.

"Must have been a bewilderment of some kind," said Maddox. "Not your run of the mill *I'm-not-here* potion, I can be certain of that. This is hundreds of times more potent, cast to inflict a permanent mind lapse. Any poor soul stuck in that little nook would probably stand there until he or she died and not realise what happened."

"You sure you're okay?" said Chloe, eying him suspiciously.

"We'll need to disarm that spell or we won't be able to go any further," said Maddox, standing up on wobbly legs. "Any chance you can shine that mobile-thing of yours and find the torch?

Chloe turned in a half circle to the right. The torch was a few feet away, teetering precariously on the edge of the channel. Maddox moved to retrieve it and spent the next few moments clicking the power button to no effect. After a vigorous shake, it came back to life. Next, he reached into his jacket pocket and produced a vial much larger than any Chloe had seen. He popped the cork and set it down gently inside the nook.

"One of these days, you'll have to tell me how you

stop those glass jars from breaking inside your pockets," said Chloe, watching him.

Maddox smiled. "It's not magic, if that's what you're thinking." He opened his jacket to reveal the dividers which had been sewn into his large inside pocket. Vials lay in four of the individual compartments, and the last space was empty.

"Are you sure you have the right one?" said Chloe, noting the vial on the floor was empty.

"It's an *Imbibing* potion," said Maddox matter-of-factly. "It will hoover-up any surface spells." He stood back, watching the vial casually, like one waiting for the kettle to boil. Chloe stood beside him, cautiously observing. Particles had begun to appear in the air around them, silver specks that danced playfully, tumbling and spinning amongst themselves like wisps of new snow. Suddenly, the innocence of the moment changed. The whirling grew more frantic—angry—as the particles were lured into the vial to be consumed by Maddox's spell. Silver dust charred to black. A moment later, the vial was full to the top with a soot-like substance. Maddox bent down and replaced the stopper.

"This vial is large enough to contain ten normal spells," he said, holding it gingerly in his hand. He set it down against the wall a few steps away. "We must remember to bring this back with us. The spell appears to have diminished, but it could still be dangerous if it were allowed back out."

"So the nook is safe?" said Chloe.

"Just a moment," said Maddox. "Remember? I said

there were two spells at work here." He scratched at his beard for a brief moment. Then, taking a step forward, spoke these words:

As the Master of Mayfair,
I'm opposed
To this terrible concoction
that's been imposed.
I'll rip and stretch you
it—you, no matter,
you've been exposed!
But first,
let me think,
What, exactly, is the opposite of closed?
Ah, yes—that's right,
the opposite of closed is
un-closed.

"Sometimes we have to write poetry in school," said Chloe, giving Maddox a look usually reserved for Dad, "but that was probably the worst thing I've ever heard. Did that silly rhyme really unlock that powerful door spell?"

"It's not silly," said Maddox defiantly.

"You just made it up, didn't you?"

"Like I said: I'm the Master of Mayfair," said Maddox. "It's not the words that matter. It's the channelling of thought that makes the spell work. The words only help to make it real."

"What exactly was it supposed to do?" said Chloe.

"It has done exactly what I asked it to do," said Maddox. "Look."

Chloe turned to look into the narrow space behind the step. A hole had appeared in the floor with stairs leading down into darkness. Maddox's counter spell had unlocked another secret.

CHAPTER 19

THE TEMPLE OF ABANDINUS

Chloe made an attempt to count the steps as they wound their way into the earth but gave up at eighty-eight, for it seemed the circling staircase would never end. Over time, her thoughts became more panicked. Was the path bewitched? Were they sentenced to travel an impossible staircase for the rest of their lives? Maddox, who was only a few steps ahead and holding the torch, seemed unconcerned by their predicament, as if he had woken that morning expecting to be crawling into the depths of the earth.

Chloe was about to voice her fears when they came around one final turn and the space grew brighter. A glow like blue moonlight illuminated a cavernous grey stone hall. The light shone brightest from beyond an arch in the wall ahead.

Chloe stared, arms loose at her sides. "What is this place?"

Maddox was beside her, his mild manner replaced by awe. "I wish I knew," he said. "This is truly miraculous."

Chloe peered up into the darkness above their heads. Somewhere, up there, was London.

"I can't believe this is here," she said. "How could it stay hidden?"

"We're down deep," said Maddox. "Deeper than the Tube. Deeper than all those silly basement swimming pools. This place, whatever it is, has been here for a long time. Longer than I can imagine. Perhaps even longer than the city itself."

"Right, but how did it get here? Who made it?" said Chloe. "Tyburn or Abandinus?"

"Tyburn was just a magician," said Maddox. "I find it difficult to believe he had anything to do with it."

"Abandinus then," said Chloe. "What was it Miss Curzon called him?"

"A *Primeval*," said Maddox flatly.

"Right," said Chloe. "She never fully explained. I have no idea what that is."

"One of the Old Ones," said Maddox. "Magicians with extremely large realms, they were powerful wielders of Old Magic. Magic many times stronger than any possessed by a London magician. Probably capable of things even I would deem impossible. Some may have been rulers or had worshipers, with minions and apprentices. I wish I could tell you more, but that's all I know. All anyone really knows." He turned toward the arch. "Shall we go see what we can find?"

They walked forward cautiously. To the left, a shelf of rock overhung the cavern floor, concealing a large dark space. Maddox paid it little attention, instead focusing on the archway ahead.

Chloe had seen temples in some of her history books. They seemed ridiculous at that moment, for nothing could have prepared her for the temple of Abandinus. It was a grand, breathtaking space. Four massive columns of stone, each seemingly capable of supporting the weight of London, had been cast in swirling patterns. From the armpit of each column, an opening had been cut from the wall, allowing torrents of water to flow through four stone ducts. Each flew outward at a dangerous trajectory, turning sharply toward the rear of the temple. Here, their waters mixed into a single cascade that fell to a reservoir below. Near the entrance, several metres from where they stood, a wide staircase rose to a dais surrounded on three sides by shimmering pools. Each danced with an otherworldly radiance, providing the temple's light.

"The skill of the hand that created this ..." said Maddox, his face awash in the soft glow from the pools. "I can't believe it exists in my realm. In all my years, I've never caught a single whiff of it. A place like this should be known. A legend. A rumour at least. Nothing. Not even Miss Curzon knew of it."

Chloe's attention remained fixed on their surroundings. It made thinking of anything else difficult.

"The person strong enough to make this wanted it to stay a secret," she said. "I don't think you should feel bad."

Maddox turned and smiled. "You're a wise apprentice

indeed," he said. "Thank you. Your words make a lot of sense, and I agree. But it's not the existence of the temple that troubles me. It's the unknowing. All of this. All that we've seen. I realise there's a lot about magic I don't understand."

Maddox inspected the staircase for traps. When he was satisfied it was safe, they climbed the dais cautiously. An area of patterned tiles lay at the top, each marked with lines similar to those on the temple columns. At the rear of the space, a stone obelisk stood like a lonely, forgotten thing. It was nearly as tall as Maddox and approximately two metres wide. At its flat top, a shallow bowl was set into the stone. Yet the most distinguishing feature of the strange object was the hole in its front: an iron lever had been set inside. Chloe and Maddox stared.

"What do you think will happen if we pull that lever?" said Chloe.

"Don't touch a thing," said Maddox. "That mechanism is far too obvious to be of any good."

"Well, it has to be for something," said Chloe.

Maddox circled the obelisk like a boxer circling his opponent. "I believe it best if we discover what that is before we start pulling levers."

Chloe moved a few paces ahead toward the shimmering pool at the head of the dais. It was larger and deeper than those on either side. Clouds of light swirled in the water, a time lapse of stormy skies. Creeping closer to the edge, she peered down. "There's something in the water!"

"What is it?" said Maddox, poking his head out from behind the obelisk.

"Stairs. I think," said Chloe.

Maddox approached. "Stairs?"

"You can see them leading down—just there," said Chloe, pointing.

Maddox looked down into the swirling water. "Fancy a swim?"

"You're joking," said Chloe.

"Of course I am," said Maddox. "However, I believe you've just discovered the purpose of the mechanism within the obelisk."

Chloe gave Maddox a blank look.

"The lever drains the water in the pool so one can access the stairs," said Maddox.

"That's it?" said Chloe looking back at the obelisk.

"It's a trap, as we suspected," said Maddox, eyes still on the water. "One of us needs to pull this lever. Obviously that's me."

"Why would you do that?" said Chloe.

Maddox moved to the front of the obelisk and shone the torch inside the opening. "I sense some deviousness in this, but I don't see any blades or darts. It appears to be a simple lever. But we both know that's not true."

"I thought you said this was far too obvious to be of any good?" said Chloe.

"I did say that."

"We could use a potion to protect you," said Chloe.

"I haven't brought anything suitable for this situation," said Maddox, shaking his head. "But I do have this." He rummaged inside his jacket pocket and handed Chloe a vial.

"Chip Sauce?" said Chloe, reading the crude label. "Do you ever stop thinking of food?"

"Wait," said Maddox. "I've given you the wrong one." He took the vial back from Chloe and swapped it with another marked *Cure for Collywobbles*. "Please give this to me if something happens."

"A stomach remedy?" said Chloe.

"That potion is a cure for many things, *collywobbles* included," said Maddox. "Just do as I say. Now, are we all set?"

"Wait. What's happening?" said Chloe crossly. "I don't want you to do this. Why would you put your hand in something you know is a trap? I almost lost you at the entrance. I can only imagine what this weird thing will do. How do you know it's safe?"

"I don't," said Maddox mildly.

"Then why do it?"

"Look around us," said Maddox. "All of the elements of this temple are here for a purpose. It's practically spelled out for us. Whoever enters is meant to pull this lever. It's the only way we're going to be able to unlock its secret."

"Will it be worth it if it ends up killing you?" Chloe shot back.

Maddox took a deep breath, looked at Chloe, then back at the obelisk. "If it helps us learn what happened to Ixworth? Yes."

Slowly, he moved his hand into the opening.

Chloe held her breath expecting to hear the whirring of blades—or worse—as the contraption did its work.

"I've almost got the handle," said Maddox. "So far so good."

Chloe allowed herself a breath.

Suddenly, the opening to the obelisk slammed tight, trapping Maddox's arm.

"Maddox!" Chloe shrieked, running to his side.

"Relax, my dear. I'm fine," said Maddox. "The opening has only closed over my arm. I believe this to be the intended purpose of the obelisk, to trap those attempting to use it."

Chloe reached out to try to pry open the trap's cover with her fingers.

"Best not touch it," said Maddox. "I'm certain it will be tamper proof."

"So you're just going to stand there with your arm trapped?" said Chloe, trying her best to sound calm. "We need to get you out."

"Let's not be so hasty," said Maddox. "Perhaps we need to play this out."

"I don't know what that's supposed to mean," said Chloe.

"We're here for answers," said Maddox, "and seeing as my arm is already stuck, I don't see why I shouldn't pull the lever within. Like you said, it has to be for something."

Chloe leant close to him. His jacket had the faintest scent of lavender. Such an ordinary thing in such an extraordinary place. The scent was reassuring. It made Maddox seem more real.

"I'm scared," she said, touching his arm. "What if it's just part of the trap—what if something bad happens to you?"

Maddox turned to her and smiled. "Trust me. I have a good feeling all will work out in the end."

Maddox pulled the lever down.

A low rumble rose from below, a sigh like that of a slumbering beast. The dais shuddered. A gigantic mechanism shifted beneath their feet. Chloe watched as the glowing pool beyond the obelisk began to froth and churn.

"The water's draining away!" Chloe cried.

"I can't see," said Maddox, craning his head from behind the obelisk. "What?"

"The pool—beside you," said Chloe.

Maddox made several more moves attempting to see around the obelisk, but his arm was caught deep, halfway between the elbow and shoulder. "You'll need to be my eyes for the remainder of this," he said.

Chloe watched as the last of the glowing water gurgled noisily away, like the emptying of a bathtub, through two narrow openings near the pool bottom. A slender staircase led down to the entrance of an arched passageway directly below the obelisk.

Chloe returned to Maddox's side. "There's a tunnel underneath us," she said. "Is it another trap?"

Maddox was silent for a moment. "I don't think so," he said after a moment. "It must be the way to the mask." He grimaced with discomfort.

"What's wrong?" said Chloe.

"The entrapment is quite tight," said Maddox. "I'm just a bit stiff."

"What can I do to help you?" said Chloe.

"I don't believe you can do anything—at least until we've solved this puzzle."

Chloe looked at Maddox's arm, buried in the obelisk.

"I still don't understand what this means," said Chloe. "Why do you think the mask is here?"

"Remember what Blythe told us?" said Maddox. "He was taken to a place like a dungeon. He heard a sound like rushing water. He was here."

"But it doesn't make any sense," said Chloe. "The temple traps anyone who drains the pool. How would anyone ever get the mask?"

Maddox thought for a moment. "Unless that's the point. One person isn't supposed to retrieve it. You need two people. One person to be the victim, the other ..."

Chloe looked at Maddox huddled in front of the obelisk. The collar of his jacket was scuffed from the entrapment. "The person in the hood brought Mr. Blythe here, didn't they?" she said.

"Yes," said Maddox.

"Blythe was trapped—like you."

"Precisely," said Maddox. "Which means the only way for me to get out of this mess is to retrieve the mask."

"But how is the mask going to help you escape?" said Chloe.

Maddox's eyes came alight. "I believe this temple was designed to carry out a sequence of events. The traps on the surface were put in place to keep out those who may stumble upon the entrance. But the actual temple was built to be a trap in itself."

"So Tyburn lured people down into the temple to turn them into old people?" said Chloe. "Why would he do that?"

Maddox stared beyond the obelisk in the direction of the drained pool. "Chloe …" he said, the worry in his voice unmistakable, "be a good sparrow, take the torch and go fetch the mask. I believe it would be in our best interest if we remove ourselves from this situation as soon as possible."

Without a word, Chloe took the torch from Maddox's jacket pocket and hurried to the edge of the pool. She descended the stairs swiftly, taking care to avoid slipping on the wet stone. In a breath, she was at the bottom, the entrance to the mysterious passage looming to her left. Switching on the torch, she rushed into darkness.

The torchlight illuminated a narrow passage of stone tiles with strange markings. From all sides, Chloe could feel the heavy thrum of water somewhere nearby, waiting to return to the pool in a rush. She wondered where it had all gone and suddenly feared Maddox flinching at the obelisk, pulling the lever and flooding the passageway. She quickened her pace.

Ahead was something curious. The soft circle of the torch beam shimmered and broke. Something was moving. Chloe took three steps closer and heard the soft sigh of falling water. She passed her fingers through a curtain of glimmering white. A waterfall. Something lay beyond, fixed to a wall of stone.

Tyburn's Mask.

Chloe reached her arm through the curtain, feeling the icy bite of the water, touching the mask with frozen fingers. It was cold. Lifting it gently, she drew it from its peg on the wall, letting it fall into her hands like she was meant to own it. The torch illuminated its grim face, a thin mouth drawn wide, slightly downturned in a frown on one side; upturned and smiling on the other. The eyes were small and round. Along both cheeks were markings that resembled a pine branch or feather.

Somebody was calling.

Chloe retreated back down the passage with the mask tight in her hand. She stopped in the shadow of the entrance, heart racing. Somebody was standing at the top of the staircase overlooking the pool.

"Ahh, there you are, Miss Ashley," said Mr. Ixworth. "I see you've brought me my mask."

CHAPTER 20

THE TYBURN MASK

"Ixworth! You're here!" Chloe cried in disbelief. She rushed from the passage and stopped at the bottom of the staircase. "We thought you had been kidnapped. What happened to you?"

"So many things since last we spoke," Ixworth replied. "I can explain, but first, I think you should come up here. Maddox has gotten himself stuck."

Chloe began climbing the stairs up from the pool. From the top of the staircase, Ixworth gazed down at her through strangely darkened eyes. She tried to read his expression.

"Do you know how to free Maddox?" she said. "Maddox!" she called. "Ixworth's here! Did you see?"

"I'm afraid he can't hear you," said Ixworth gravely. "He's unconscious."

"What happened to him?" said Chloe, stopping near the top of the staircase.

"I think he blacked out from his struggles at the obelisk," said Ixworth. "I see you have my mask."

Chloe looked down at *Tyburn's Mask,* clutched firmly in her hand. The face seemed happier than it had a moment ago in the passage. "Your mask?" she said.

"Yes, I'll explain," said Ixworth, holding out his hand, "but there's no time to waste. Come up here."

"Are you okay?" said Chloe, "you're acting funny."

Ixworth's face contorted strangely and his expression changed to something Chloe had never seen in him before. Anger.

"Enough with all this talking," he spat. "Come up here now!"

Chloe retreated slowly down the staircase. Her hands trembled. Something was wrong with Ixworth. She suddenly remembered what Miss Curzon had said about the *Greave Note*. About Ixworth being its victim. Had it made him crazy?

"I'm losing my patience, Miss Ashley," Ixworth snarled. "Do I need to come and take my mask from you?"

"Why do you keep calling it *your* mask?" Chloe said, trying hard to sound confident. "Wasn't it made by Abandinus—or Tyburn?"

Ixworth laughed mockingly. "Tyburn was just a desperate fool who stumbled upon this place. His fame far surpassed his abilities. No simple magician could ever create this temple. It was even a strain for Abandinus. It took everything he had to build it."

"I don't even know what this place is for," said Chloe.

Ixworth appeared confused. "Isn't that why you're here? For the mask?"

"We came to find you," said Chloe. "Not some silly temple."

"Silly?" said Ixworth. "I don't think you realise what

you've discovered. This place was built with Old Magic. It works together with the mask. The temple is the power source; the mask is the syphon, taking the magic of any who wear it and then passing it along to the next. The cycle repeats. Over and over. Take from one. Give to another. That was Abandinus's plan—Tyburn's too. Lure magicians into the temple trap. Take their magic. Eventually they would own all of London's realms. But now that is my destiny. I've already taken Blythe's. Maddox is next."

"Don't you touch him!" Chloe cried.

"I'll do as I wish," said Ixworth.

"Why would you hurt your best friend?" said Chloe. "You're not thinking straight, Ixworth. It must be the *Greave Note*. The one Miss Curzon told us about it. It's making you act crazy!"

Ixworth, scoffed. "I don't know what a *Greave Note* is," he said. "But if you're referring to Blythe and Thirsk's little plan to bewitch me into doing their bidding, then clearly that backfired."

"So they were the ones that gave you the *Greave Note*?" said Chloe.

"Those two have been working together to try to expand their realms," Ixworth said angrily. "Thirsk has been offing magicians for years, and Blythe was tired of listening to the Magician's Guild. They thought the mask would be the perfect tool. Blythe suspected it was hidden in Maddox's realm, so he coerced me into helping them. I don't know how. I had no choice but to obey. They told me to find the mask for them. Maddox would never suspect nor notice me searching his realm. It took me and my brownies weeks. Scouring the banks of the River Tyburn, inch by inch."

"So you made the secret passage in the workshop," said Chloe. "And the pushpin map! It was your house I ended up in."

Ixworth's eyes narrowed. "Yes, I heard you were snooping about in my house. I'm surprised Maddox let you use the hat racks. If I'd known, I would have cast an *Eviction* to stop you as well."

Ixworth edged closer to the top of the stairs. Chloe retreated another step back. She didn't know what to do. Her only thought was to distract him. "Why did you kidnap Blythe?"

"I know what you're up to, Miss Ashley," Ixworth said menacingly. "Keeping me talking will not stop me from taking my mask."

"So you're just a murderer now?" said Chloe angrily.

"I haven't murdered anybody," he said. "Yet."

"We saw Blythe. We know what you did to him," said Chloe.

"Yes, you did," said Ixworth. "You can imagine my surprise when I discovered you had broken into another house that I owned."

"How is Blythe's house yours?" said Chloe.

"All of his realm is mine," said Ixworth. "I took it from him. But don't go blaming me for that. It was his own fault."

"How is it someone else's fault if you steal from them?" said Chloe.

"After my brownies discovered the temple of Abandinus, he came here willingly."

"So Blythe was lying?" said Chloe. "He said someone kidnapped him and forced the mask on him."

"It doesn't take a scholar to know Blythe is a liar," said Ixworth. "Obviously he wanted your help getting the mask back."

"But why would you use it on him in the first place?" said Chloe. "You're not like that."

"It was Blythe's idea," Ixworth sneered. "Like I said: he and I came here together. I had no choice but to lead him. But he didn't understand the purpose of this place. He used the lever in the obelisk. He thought it would unlock the mask. And after becoming trapped, he realised the mask lay within the pool. I was ordered to fetch it. Such a strange twist of fate. If only he wasn't so greedy and thought things through, maybe things would have ended differently. If only he had understood."

"Understood what?" said Chloe.

Ixworth looked at her fiercely. "How the *Tyburn Mask* works. After retrieving it from the tunnel, I gave it to Blythe. He wore it first. The fool. And he paid a terrible price. It consumed every drop of his magic. Everything. It's a miracle he's still alive. And even then he still didn't understand. He thought I had tricked him into wearing the mask first. Then he ordered me to wear it. He was hoping it would drain my magic and that I would be foolish enough to give it back to him. But I was no longer under his control. The mask was more powerful than whatever he was using to control me."

The darkness around Ixworth's eyes seemed to have grown darker. "Now, enough with this chatter," he said, taking a step toward Chloe. "Miss Ashley, you have ten seconds to come up here with the mask or I will issue a *Pandation* that will fold Maddox in half. And then I will do the same to you. I wish I were joking. This is non-negotiable."

Frantic, Chloe scanned the pool, desperate to find something to help: a weapon, a stone to throw. Perhaps she could charge up the stairs, startle Ixworth and free Maddox. But then she realised how futile all of it was. She wouldn't be able to do any of it. Ixworth had them. She couldn't miraculously save the day. All she had was the mask.

"Five seconds!" shouted Ixworth.

"Okay, okay," said Chloe, "I'm coming up. Please don't hurt Maddox."

Chloe climbed the stairs, her breath ragged, the mask nearly slipping from her shaking hands. Ixworth watched her approach, eyes narrowed.

As Chloe reached the top of the staircase, she could see Maddox slumped against the obelisk, his arm still trapped tight. Suddenly he stirred.

"Did you hurt, Maddox?" said Chloe, trying to distract Ixworth.

"He's only stunned," said Ixworth, eyes still on her.

"Is he okay?" said Chloe.

"It doesn't matter," said Ixworth.

Maddox stood up suddenly. With his free hand, he removed his last remaining potion from his inside pocket, and with one quick motion, hurled it at the unsuspecting Ixworth. Chloe watched it fly, a clear sparkling thing.

Ixworth drew a quick hand in defence, raising his flattened palm in an attempt to deflect the speeding dart. The vial shattered, covering his hand in an amber liquid.

"Run, Chloe!" Maddox cried from the obelisk.

Ixworth lunged toward Chloe, but Maddox's potion began to take effect. The liquid expanded outward, bursting like a fat milkweed, encasing Ixworth's arm in a thick, batter-like substance.

Chloe froze. She didn't know what to do. Run or help Maddox? She scurried back down the steps of the pool, not knowing what to do.

"Pathetic," Ixworth sneered angrily, staring at the pillowy substance that was growing up his arm. He made a wild motion with the fingers of his free hand. "Your magic is feeble, Maddox."

Chip Sauce came apart in tiny particles of golden dust.

Ixworth turned his attention to Chloe, who had reached the passage at the bottom of the empty pool. "That's far enough, Miss Ashley," he said. "There's nowhere for you to go. And I still have Maddox. Bring me my mask."

Frightened, Chloe retreated to the passage at the bottom of the pool. She thought suddenly of Mum and Dad, working, or whatever it was they spent their days doing. They wouldn't even realise she was gone until much later. There was no hope of rescue. If the temple had been hidden for a thousand years, it was sure to remain so for a thousand more. She wanted to speak but was afraid fear and anger would mince her words.

"Let Maddox go," she called.

"There is no way out of this," Ixworth shouted back.

Chloe ran her hand along the face of the mask. It was still cold. "I'll smash this mask beneath my foot!"

"I'll fold your Maddox into a coffin if you don't bring it to me now!" Ixworth raged.

Chloe stifled a cry, stung by Ixworth's cruel tone.

"Have you lost your mind?" Maddox called weakly from behind Ixworth.

Ixworth paced for a few moments, muttering to himself, then returned to the top of the staircase. "She won't leave here until I get the mask," he bellowed.

"And once you have that—what next?" called Maddox.

Ixworth turned his full attention to Maddox: "I'll help the mask fulfil its purpose. To take the magic of every remaining magician in London. Starting with you."

"This is insane," said Maddox. "Listen to yourself. You sound like a mad man."

"The mask needs to feed," Ixworth muttered to himself. He turned his attention again to Chloe. "Last chance Chloe. Bring me my mask."

Chloe stood in the door to the passage, the mask in her hand. Its lopsided face appeared happy one instant, angry the next. There was nothing to be done. She couldn't hide forever. Handing over the mask was the only option.

And then, a thought popped into Chloe's head quite unexpectedly. Blythe had thought he had been tricked into wearing the mask first. If only he had understood the way the magic worked. The order of its operation. Take from one. Give to another. Over and over. Chloe knew what had to be done. Turning, she ducked back into the safety of the passage, and then taking a deep breath, placed the *Tyburn Mask* over her face.

Chloe suddenly witnessed the mask's dark history playing out before her eyes. The warlock Abandinus and his evil ways, chased from his home by a powerful army. His arrival in old London, tired and spent from being so long without a realm. And then using his remaining energy and vast knowledge of Old Magic to create the mask and the temple in an attempt to regain his former might. His creation would sidestep the natural laws of magic and allow him to steal from others. To take their realms in an instant. And then, Abandinus was gone, and the story fast forwarded to Tyburn and his discovery of the temple. His greed and desperation for power. The vile things he did. The magicians he lured and trapped. And then finally to Ixworth, reluctantly taking Blythe's magic. The terrible grip the mask had on him and all who wore it. Chloe witnessed it all.

And when the story had played out, a deathly chill washed over her. She felt the mask's angry presence rummaging through her bones and nerves. Searching for what it desired. Magic. Finding Chloe's tiny plant-ruining *Rosebud,* it gobbled it down ravenously. Chloe should have been sad at her loss. She had worked so hard to learn that one spell. Yet as she removed the mask, she could still feel its presence, like a comforting old friend. *You only need to think about me,* the mask whispered. *Only me.* And Chloe agreed. She craved to wear it again, and above all, to serve. Serve the mask! Abandinus was gone. But the mask remained. And it needed her help carrying out its purpose: to steal the magic and might of every London magician for its long dead master.

"Time's up!"

Ixworth grabbed her wrist. In her dazed state, she hadn't seen him descend the staircase. He tore the mask from her grip.

"Give it back. It's mine!" she shouted.

Ixworth let her go, turning back toward the stairs.

"You're being ridiculous," he said. Chloe tried to chase after him, but her legs were weak and wobbly from her ordeal. She hobbled slowly up the stairs and then collapsed at the top.

Ixworth had nearly reached the obelisk. Maddox watched him approach, making no move to defend himself.

"Don't do this," he said tiredly.

Ixworth's eyes seemed to be gone, replaced by the strange shadowy darkness.

"It's already done," he said. Stepping forward, he fitted the mask over Maddox's face. For the briefest of moments, the mask shone brightly, then it grew dull. Maddox slumped forward, his arm still held tightly in the trap.

For a moment, Ixworth stood staring at his fallen friend, his expression confused. Then he removed the mask gently from Maddox and placed it over his own face.

The Temple of Abandinus groaned, suddenly weighted by magical energies that had begun to spin in the space between the massive columns. Below the dais, the pools emitted webs of energy, weaving furiously through the charged atmosphere, their spidery fingers coming to rest on top of the obelisk.

Ixworth realised something was wrong. He clawed at the mask, trying to tear it free. But the mask had him in its grip and was desperate to fulfil its terrible purpose. Ravenous, it rooted through the rich soil of his magic, and finding it deep, devoured it greedily. Ixworth fell forward, his body twitching. After a moment, he lay still, the mask beside him.

The trap in the obelisk sprang open, releasing Maddox. For a moment he stood blinking like he couldn't quite believe he had been set free.

"You tricked him," he said looking at Chloe. "The mask has taken his magic."

He stood for a moment longer, pondering his predicament. And then suddenly, the mask took its dark hold, and Maddox's desire to own the mask sent him racing to retrieve it from where it lay. In a moment it was in his hand.

"It's mine!" he cried in a strange un-Maddox-like voice.

Chloe scrambled clumsily toward Maddox, her craving for the mask like a fire behind her eyes. But something was happening. The mask had begun to glow as intense as a white-hot star. Maddox yelped, letting it go. It fell solidly to the temple floor where it continued to glow, the circle of light around it bulging outward. Around the dais, the temple shook and groaned in protest. Chloe watched in horror as Tyburn's mask began to crumble. Tiny grains of a windswept sandcastle. In an instant it was gone, a blackened smear the only evidence it had ever been. Around them, the temple suddenly fell silent. The shimmering pools grew pale. The water-filled ducts stopped their timeless flow.

Chloe and Maddox looked at each other dumbfounded.

"What happened?" said Chloe.

"The *Tyburn Mask* is no more," said Maddox with a heavy sigh. "For that, I'm very grateful. I really wasn't feeling myself after wearing it. I don't know what came over me. I believe you and I were in its grip. And behaving badly, I might add."

Chloe nodded and came to stand beside him. "That mask was making me crazy."

"I think the mask makes everyone crazy," said Maddox. "Anyone and everyone who wears it." He turned to look at Chloe. "You tricked Ixworth into stealing his own magic. That was very foolish of you.

You didn't know what that mask would do. You could have been killed."

"I did know," said Chloe. "The idea came from Blythe. He accused Ixworth of doing the same thing to him."

Maddox looked at Chloe thoughtfully. "Ixworth never guessed. He didn't know you were a budding magician, did he?"

"Well, I was a magician," said Chloe. "I gave my *Rosebud* to you."

Maddox looked thoughtful. "Not a bad spell either. I think you have great potential. Sadly, you'll need to start your lessons at the beginning."

"I'll study harder," said Chloe.

"I think my feelings are a little hurt," said the voice of Ixworth from behind them. "Why didn't you tell me Chloe was practising to be a magician?"

Chloe and Maddox whirled around.

"Get behind me," said Maddox, holding his arm out.

Ixworth approached slowly. "You have nothing to fear from me any longer," he said, holding up his hands. Ixworth's appearance had changed: his face was more lined, his hair thinner, the grey more prominent. But the darkness about his eyes had completely vanished. "How did you destroy the mask?" he said shakily.

"I'm not exactly sure," said Maddox.

"Are you ... you?" said Chloe cautiously.

Ixworth smiled tiredly. "I think so."

"And the *Greave Note?*" said Chloe.

"I don't know what that is," said Ixworth.

"A powerful spell created with Old Magic," said

Maddox. "I found one in your jacket pocket. Miss Curzon said you had been cursed with it. Someone had hidden the spell in a copy of the *Quarterly Crow*."

"Blythe and Thirsk," Ixworth said heavily. "This *Greave Note* must be how they were controlling me. I wasn't sure how or what it was, but I had no choice but to do as they asked. They made me search Mayfair for the *Tyburn Mask* behind your back, Maddox."

Maddox nodded gravely. "Two or more magicians would be needed to create one," he said.

Ixworth was quiet for a moment, his ordeal clearly weighing heavy on him. "I'm so sorry for all that I've done to you both," he said after a moment. "And Chloe—especially you. I must have frightened you. I didn't mean it. Please believe me."

Chloe noted the sad look on Ixworth's face. "I think … I understand," she said, remembering how much she had yearned for the mask herself. "Not everything. I'm still confused about some things that happened." She took a step toward Ixworth. "It's okay. I can forgive you."

Ixworth smiled, tears sparkling in his eyes. She had never seen a grown-up cry before.

Maddox was looking at the black stain near their feet. It was all that remained of *Tyburn's Mask*. "Old Magic against Old Magic," he said.

Chloe and Ixworth looked at him dumbly.

"Chloe and I saw Blythe," Maddox said, looking up at Ixworth. "He was drained of all of his magic and could barely stand. But you …"

"Yes," said Ixworth, looking down at his hands. "I

am altered. Tyburn's Mask took some of my magic. But not all."

"So Miss Curzon was wrong," said Maddox.

"What do you mean?" said Chloe, puzzled.

Maddox smiled. "She said nothing good would come from using the *Tyburn Mask*. Yet clearly something has."

"I still don't understand?" said Chloe.

"The first time Ixworth wore the mask, it was giving him magic from Blythe. But the second time, the mask was taking from Ixworth. Drawing magic in, including that powerful *Greave Note*. All that potent Old Magic filled it up and only took half of his normal magic. The mask saved his life. It cured Ixworth of the *Greave Note*."

"But what happened to the mask?" said Chloe.

"Old Magic and Old Magic don't mix," said Maddox. "Miss Curzon said a *Greave Note* is nearly impossible to control and very unstable. What's the saying? Adding fuel to the fire? The *Mask* and the *Greave Note* must have destroyed one another."

Chloe frowned and looked from Ixworth to Maddox. "I still have so many questions," she said, "about all of this."

Maddox smiled. "And they shall be answered. Come you two. Let's retreat to a more comfortable place. As Blythe suggested, this temple is beginning to remind me of a dungeon."

✦ ✦ ✦

"So who made the hat racks?" said Chloe some hours later after the three friends had returned to the curiosity shop. Maddox had laid bare his cupboards and conjured a most magnificent tea to celebrate the return of Ixworth.

"I did, of course," said Ixworth.

"I thought as much," said Maddox. "Only you and your *Flexure* could come up with something as clever as those hat racks."

"But what were they for?" said Chloe. "And why couldn't Maddox sniff out the one in the workshop?"

"I've been perfecting my hat racks for years," Ixworth explained, "using a discreet *Flexure* so they would avoid detection. It was a hobby at first, but I recently started using them to investigate my mother's death."

"But I thought your mother died of an illness?" said Maddox.

"That is true to an extent," said Ixworth. "As you know, Blythe was angry that half of his father's realm was passed to my mother. He wanted it back. For a long time, I'd suspected he had something to do with her illness. Mother suffered for years with a strange disease resistant to the strongest potions and alchemy. It was terrible. And then ..." Ixworth's voice faded, and it was a moment before he was able to speak again. "Shortly after her death, I received an unsigned postcard from the Magdalen Islands, sending regards and sympathies. It stood out. I remember it clearly. I never understood who it was from. But then, when I found out Blythe had a *Charmian Cabbage* growing in his home—the rarest plant there is—it was too much of a coincidence. *Charmian Cabbages* only grow in one place."

"The Magdalen Islands!" cried Maddox.

"That's right," said Ixworth sadly. "When Blythe commissioned us to craft the windowsill greenhouse—as he put it—to accommodate a rare specimen, I knew he did it. The *Charmian Cabbage's* poison is undetectable. He was taunting me. He wanted me to know he was the one who'd murdered my mother."

"The *Greave Note* said something about cabbage soup," said Chloe. "Remember, Maddox? There was a story about two magicians who died from eating it at one of Blythe's parties."

Maddox stroked at his beard. "Yes, that's right. Miss Curzon mentioned the *Greave Note* reveals a terrible truth. Even if the words themselves make no sense. This must have been what set you off, Ixworth. The *Greave Note* was telling you Blythe was responsible for your mother's death."

Ixworth nodded sadly, but didn't respond.

Maddox shifted uncomfortably. "So you created the hat racks to sneak into Blythe's?"

"Yes," said Ixworth flatly. "I know Blythe and his scheming ways. I had my busyness craft offerings I knew would appeal to him. I only wanted him to take the hat rack. As expected, he wanted the *Memory Desk* and the *Wherebox*." Ixworth paused, looking at Chloe and then Maddox. "I'm sorry I didn't tell you. But there were moments I thought I was mad—or paranoid. I didn't want you to think I was crazy. Otherwise, I would have asked for your help."

Maddox clapped Ixworth on the shoulder. "You have nothing to apologise for," he said smiling. "What

Blythe put you through was terrible. And I think you're a better man than me. I doubt I would have kept him around after what he did to you."

Ixworth looked down toward his feet sheepishly. "Honestly," he said, "my plan for Blythe was not a noble one. We all know the influence of the mask, how it controls us. I was going to use it on Thirsk next. He and Blythe were business partners, intent on taking over all of London's realms. When Blythe went missing, Thirsk started looking for him. He made many attempts to break into my house. I think he eventually figured out I was keeping Blythe a prisoner. That's when he came for me."

"Chloe and I witnessed that exchange," said Maddox. "That was quite a display of magic, Ixworth."

"Yes," said Ixworth. "With Blythe's magic added to my own, I could achieve far more than I ever thought possible."

"Why was Thirsk following me, then?" said Chloe looking at Ixworth. "Maddox had to give me something to chase him away."

Ixworth massaged his temples. "He knew you and I were associates. I'm guessing he hoped to question you. To see if you knew something."

The three sat sipping their tea for a long moment, each trying to come to terms with all they had suffered.

"I just have one last question," said Chloe as she considered a final half-scone. "Why did you have so many hat racks? You had one in the workshop, three in your house, one in the park."

Ixworth gave her a curious look.

"I'm not sure what you mean," he said. "I've been using hat racks to get around since Maddox and I opened this shop. You really don't expect a magician to walk anywhere, do you?"

◆ ◆ ◆

The memory of the *Tyburn Mask* stayed with Chloe for many weeks. Its terrible voice in her head, its grim history playing out again and again. The full extent of Ixworth's loss had yet to be measured.

"I feel like I've misplaced half of myself," he would joke dryly from time to time.

Chloe suspected there was more truth to this than he was letting on. She would watch him as he busied about after coming back to assist in the shop's reopening. There was a sadness to him like he was hiding something unspeakable inside. At times, she wanted to ask him how he was feeling, but she knew Ixworth wasn't the chatty type. He wasn't like Maddox. It would make him uncomfortable to talk about it. And he had suffered enough.

One Friday, Chloe accompanied Maddox to Mr. Blythe's house in Holland Park. When they arrived, they discovered the gate to the front yard had been left open. Beyond, the hedge rows had grown wild. A brownie dressed in a smock and worker's britches opened the door before Maddox could knock.

"Good morning, Mr. Maddox," the brownie said brightly.

"Good morning," said Maddox, "you must be one of Ixworth's busyness?"

The brownie bowed low, extending a small arm to usher them inside. They stepped into the front hall, and Chloe closed the door behind them.

"Ixworth asked that we collect his things—books, hat racks and whatnot—and return home," said the brownie. "He won't be spending any more time on these premises."

Maddox nodded, giving the hallway a cursory glance as if looking for something.

"Have you any news of Mr. Blythe?" he asked.

"None sir," said the brownie sadly. "We were tending to him, but then two days ago, he disappeared."

"Right-right," said Maddox. "I was just wondering if he might have returned for a few of his things." He turned to Chloe. "He must have gone to one of his other residences. I wonder how he escaped?"

Chloe shrugged. She wasn't the vengeful type, but after all the things he had done, there was a part of her that felt Blythe deserved what had happened to him.

On the way home, the streets were sleepier than their usual summer selves, and Wood's Mews greeted her with the sound of crickets instead of the hellos of neighbours. Upon reaching her front door, Chloe hesitated, checking twice to make sure it was locked. She had been wondering if Thirsk had been released from the hospital. He had been badly injured in his encounter with Ixworth. Nonetheless, the thought of him creeping the streets of London again made her shiver.

Chloe found the jewellery box after a moment of searching in her bedroom. She had tucked it behind a stack of books on her nightstand. *The Darkening of Nicholas Mallow* remained at the front: her favourite book from Ixworth. The story's climax took place atop a precarious clifftop. The villain, Maulgyn, there became ensnared in wild vines and fell to his death in the Witherwind River. After reading it, Chloe thought it was such a conclusive ending, yet in light of recent events, her opinion had changed. Was Maulgyn truly gone? Perhaps he had survived the fall and swam to a far shore of the Witherwind to seek revenge on poor Nicholas in the next book. Chloe opened the front flap of the book and then closed it again. Endings in real life were different from the ones in storybooks. There were so many unanswered questions in real life. What would happen to the withered Mr. Blythe and his realm? Would Thirsk keep trying to take over all of London's realms? Would Ixworth ever be okay after suffering both a *Greave Note* and the *Tyburn Mask*?

✦ ✦ ✦

Autumn was approaching. Chloe received her timetable for school that week. She felt sad she wouldn't be visiting the shop as much. Some of the events that summer had been frightening, but she would miss Ixworth and Maddox. She told them so on that Thursday when she showed up at the shop. Ixworth still looked tired, despite claiming to have made a full recovery, and was determined to keep busy. His busyness of brownies was already hard at work on a number of new and extraordinary things.

"We'll miss having you about as well," said Maddox sadly. "You'll still come by when you can, right? After we reopen?"

"Of course," said Chloe. "Do you really think I could spend time in a normal shop after all that's happened?"

"It might be less dangerous," Ixworth said thoughtfully.

"I think I can handle it," said Chloe, smiling.

Just then, Mr. Winch came in from the store room.

"I was wondering if I could bother one of you for a moment?" he said, looking at Ixworth and then Maddox.

"Yes-yes-yes, of course," said Maddox. "What is it?"

"I'd like to run a few things by you. I've just brought up some items for our first showing. *Tipsy-Toe-Boots*, Drink Making Stations, and a Miniature Lionhead Tower Cabin."

"Yes, of course," said Maddox. He looked at Ixworth.

"Be my guest," said Ixworth.

Chloe watched Maddox and the brownie leave.

"I never thanked you," said Ixworth after they had gone, "for helping me."

"Yes you did," said Chloe.

"It was a sad acknowledgement," said Ixworth. "You risked your life, saved me without a thought for yourself."

"You would have done the same for me," Chloe said shyly.

"Yes," said Ixworth, "without hesitation." He paused

then and was quiet for a moment. "I'm sorry for what I put you through. Maddox too. I hope you can trust me again."

Chloe had also wondered if she'd be able to trust him after all that had happened. But sitting with Ixworth in the shop, quietly chatting, felt as warm and magical as it had on the first day. She grinned wide, and Ixworth smiled back. And that's all they ever spoke of it again.

ACKNOWLEDGMENTS

I'd like to thank the following people for their kindness and support: Jennifer Musgrove, Tessa David, Sara O'Keefe, Sirah Jarocki, Paulina Wyrt, Tara Lewis and Kong Njo.

Printed in Great Britain
by Amazon